Showdown in South Africa

With the fury of their onslaught, the South African soldiers melted into the frenzied crowd like the blade of a hot and bloody knife.

Claude Hayes grabbed Paul Krudd tightly as the fleeing rioters rushed past, bumping into them in their blind retreat. Hayes stumbled under the weight of the wounded white man, and the black SOB tightened his face and grunted to squeeze more strength into his grip. He had twenty feet to go. He looked at it, and started running.

Too late.

A trooper, big and ugly, confronted him, his blood-covered truncheon poised above Claude Hayes's head. He smashed it down.

SOBs

SOME CHOOSE HELL

JACK HILD

A GOLD EAGLE BOOK FROM
W✦RLDWIDE

TORONTO •NEW YORK • LONDON • PARIS
AMSTERDAM • STOCKHOLM • HAMBURG
ATHENS • MILAN • TOKYO • SYDNEY

First edition November 1985

ISBN 0-373-61609-0

Special thanks and acknowledgment to
Robin Hardy for his contribution to this work.

Printed in Canada

1

Maj. Sidney Snider of the South African Bureau of State Security—BOSS for short—roared with anger.

"Answer the questions, black bastard!" He swung his fist and chopped the prisoner across the face. The African opened his mouth and screamed, and Snider caught his knuckles on the man's teeth.

He pulled his hand away sharply and looked at the thin line of blood oozing from the laceration.

"Terrorist fucker," he swore, his lip curling in contempt. He put his face right up beside the prisoner's and breathed against it. "We want to know how these diamonds are smuggled out of South Africa. And we're not stopping until we get the answer."

He straightened and looked at the man under interrogation. The prisoner's eyes were closed. He was breathing heavily through his open mouth. Lines of bright blood streaked his dark skin.

"Tell us!" Major Snider commanded. He slapped the prisoner's face with the flat of his hand. "Tell us!" he roared again, slapping with his other hand.

The prisoner's head bounced back and forth as the major's hands milled across his cheeks and temples. His breath became ragged. He groaned.

"Sir..." A hand reached out and held Snider's. His young assistant was obeying his instructions to remind his commanding officer that he might be going too far.

Snider stopped.

"Thank you, Jacob," he said, moving away from the prisoner. He glanced at the clock and the wall. Two P.M. He paced to the barred window of his office in the security police headquarters in Johannesburg, and considered his choices.

He was having cocktails at the Krudd estate that evening. The prime minister would be there. His colleagues who made up the Inner Circle were meeting. He wanted this business of the stolen diamonds over and done with. The Inner Circle was working on a much more important project. It was time to call in the experts.

"Jacob, I'm going out for a few hours. Have Ernie and Johann come in. I want answers from the prisoner. Tell them they have two hours."

"Yes, sir." The young assistant exited briskly.

Snider walked back to the prisoner. The black man was handcuffed to the arms of the chair and his feet were shackled in leg irons. He was naked. Snider leaned in close, his breath pushing against the prisoner's bloodied face.

"Two hours," he said slowly. "Then you'll tell us what we want to know."

A few minutes later Snider had escaped from his office and was racing his green Mercedes down the M-1 out of Johannesburg. The high-ranking major passed the yellow mountains of tailings from the city's gold mines and headed across the rolling high veldt to the neighboring city of Pretoria, capital of the South African republic.

He turned off before he entered Pretoria and drove up the side of one of the hills that surrounded the capital. At the top, commanding a view of the wind-swept landscape of the Transvaal, sat a massive, square building of stone called the Voortrekker Monument.

Major Snider left his car in the parking lot beside the tourist buses and walked up the grand ceremonial steps to the massive entrance.

He looked back at the city of Pretoria spread out in the green valley below. In the distance the rolling veldts of white-ruled Africa stretched north as far as the Limpopo River. On the other side of the water-way, in Zimbabwe and Mozambique, the enemy waited.

Black Africa. The sworn adversary of South Africa's white regime.

A short, older man with a corpulent waistline approached Snider quietly from behind. He wore an expensive suit, and a large diamond sparkled on the ring on his little finger.

"Our country is surrounded by hostile neighbors, and we have no friends in the world to help us," he said to the major, as if reading his mind.

Snider turned sharply, in surprise. He relaxed when he saw Wilhelm Krudd, a diamond industrialist and one of South Africa's wealthiest men. Krudd was a friend and ally.

"Just as in 1838, more than a hundred fifty years ago, our pioneering ancestors, the Voortrekkers, were besieged by twenty thousand Zulu warriors in the Battle of Blood River."

"It is so refreshing to be with you, Major Snider. You, more than anyone, are convinced of our inevitable victory."

Snider grinned. "Every schoolchild learns that the Voortrekkers were outnumbered forty to one. That they had one chance in a hundred of winning that battle."

"Yes," Wilhelm Krudd agreed. "The fact that they had muskets while the Zulus had spears—"

"But the victory came from God," Snider interrupted hastily. "It is the white man's destiny to rule South Africa, and the black man's destiny to serve us."

"Show me our impostor," Krudd demanded, changing the subject.

"In a moment, Wilhelm. First, let's go inside."

They went through the entrance into the giant monument's interior, letting their eyes adjust to the diminished light.

A reverent hush filled the Hall of Heroes. The walls were covered by marble sculptures of the Great Trek, stone pioneers sweating and toiling to push their covered wagons over the Drakensberg Mountains. On the other side, a great tapestry showed Zulu King Dingaan's savage warriors beating their ox-hide shields with their spears as they prepared for their charge against the beleaguered white settlers.

The floor was pierced by a large round opening, and Snider and Krudd looked down at the great stone cenotaph in its underground chamber. Around the edges of the hole, a spot of sunlight from a small opening in the dome high overhead played on the cold granite. Exactly at noon on December 16, the anniversary of the Battle of Blood River, the sunlight shone for a few moments on the cenotaph's inscription.

"We for thee, South Africa," Krudd whispered, reading the words carved in stone.

Major Snider gazed reverently at the eternal flame burning in its glass cage. "That lamp is the torch of civilization," he said to Krudd. "Which we Europeans brought to the Dark Continent, and which we keep alight against the tides of terrorism and war."

"Seven million of us against twenty-two million of them within our own borders. We're like the little Dutch boy who put his finger in the crumbling dike to save his country. But the rising tide we face is primitive Africa. I give you all the support I can, Sidney. But I admit to being discouraged at times. Now show me our impostor."

"Be it God, fate or what have you, Wilhelm. It was ordained at Blood River that the white race would lead South Africa to its destiny as a nation."

Wilhelm Krudd cleared his throat. "The impostor," he reminded the BOSS major again.

Sidney Snider swept his eyes one last time around the granite dome, the cenotaph and the stone relief of the Voortrekkers forever frozen in their epic journey.

"It was the greatest event in the history of our country," he said. "And if our project succeeds, we will have equaled it. Perhaps someday, our names and likenesses will also be carved in stone."

"Perhaps." The wealthy industrialist was clearly uncomfortable and impatient. "The impostor, Sidney. I am a busy man. Tonight the prime minister is coming to the house…"

"Yes, of course." Major Snider tore himself away from his vision of valor.

The two conspirators left the memorial and walked quickly down the long steps into the rock gardens surrounding the monument. Sidney led the way past couples meandering along the paths, until they approached the rear of the building. The only person in sight was a black gardener, carefully trimming a hedge.

"By the way," Sidney said as they walked. "We are narrowing down the inquiry regarding the diamonds being smuggled out of your mines. We know that the terrorists are smuggling them out of South Africa to the Amsterdam markets to finance their activities. The question is, how? I expect to have the answer tonight."

"Excellent, Sidney. And as far as the second matter goes, you are sure the impostor will be loyal to us?"

Sidney stopped and smiled at Krudd. "Absolutely," he said with complete conviction, as if the question had never occurred to him. He started walking again, giving a curt nod to the African gardener. "He's one of my agents," Snider explained to Krudd.

The security officer led the industrialist to a small metal door in the side of the monument. The gardener began to walk across the lawn toward them.

"I discovered our man working in a little African theater company in Transkei," said Sidney. "I immediately noticed two things about him, which inspired our plan. First, he is a natural mimic. He was able to imitate in voice, mannerism and gesture every public figure I named for him. And second of all, his looks."

"Sir!" The gardener approached them with a handful of keys.

"Open it," Snider ordered.

"Yes, sir." The gardener immediately picked a key and slipped it in the keyhole of the metal door.

"There have been no problems?" Snider asked.

"None at all, sir. 'Cept he keeps getting hungry all the time."

"As long as you keep feeding him until we're ready to use him."

"Yes, sir. I do, sir."

"Wait here until we return," Snider instructed the man. "Follow me," he told Krudd. He led the man through a narrow corridor onto the landing of a metal staircase that led deep into the earth under the Voortrekker Monument.

"An air-raid shelter!" Krudd exclaimed.

"Yes. Built in 1948 when the monument was constructed and now almost forgotten. It was intended for the use of prominent government officials in time of war. I have agents guarding it twenty-four hours a day to ensure it remains forgotten."

The two men descended the stairs. The vast underground cavern was barely illuminated by low-watt lights along the walls. At the bottom, two stories down, they found themselves in a long dusty hallway lined with doors. Snider went directly to the first one and opened it with a key. Krudd pushed in behind him, with unconcealed curiosity.

The room they walked into was like a windowless hotel suite. It was brightly lit by lamps, and a television blared.

A short, thin black man jumped up from the couch as they entered. He was clearly startled.

"Relax, Umtazi," Snider told him. "You're the bishop. This is my friend Wilhelm—"

"Yes," Wilhelm Krudd deliberately interrupted before his full name was revealed. "I'm very pleased to meet you." He extended his hand.

Almost immediately, the little man underwent a visible transformation. The features of his face seemed to melt into new expressions, and his posture was altered. He clasped Krudd's hand and spoke in a thin, high-pitched voice.

"I'm so pleased. I love my white brothers. It's so important that we work together to solve our country's terrible racial problem and put an end to apartheid."

Krudd's mouth dropped open in amazement while Snider watched with an amused smile.

"It's amazing," the diamond millionaire said, clearly astounded.

"Yes," Sidney agreed. "For a few thousand dollars, look what we have been able to buy."

"I think it will work," Krudd mused. "I think it will really work."

"Of course it will," Snider told him. "After all, God is on our side."

2

Claude Hayes stood on the wide veranda that ran along the front of his hotel and gazed out over the streets of Maputo. He conjured from memory images of the city he had left behind almost a decade ago.

It had been called Lourenco Marques then, and it had not been a pleasant place to live. Clouds of dark smoke had billowed from the western suburbs, and the orange tracers from guerrilla mortars arced across the sky on voyages of doom. The Portuguese colonial masters were in full flight, and on the eve of independence, the city had screamed and burned.

Today it bustled. Civil servants hurried in dark Western suits to offices in ministry buildings. The air reverberated with the din of trucks and cars. The avenues were lined by purple flowering jacaranda trees and crimson acacia glowing against the white stucco buildings. Claude Hayes smiled just for being back. It was nice to spend some time in Mozambique. Especially as a tourist visiting old friends instead of a warrior general at the head of a victorious guerrilla army.

The old black limousine drawing up to the curb in front of the hotel entrance was for him, and the American descended to the street. The driver, a young man in a soldier's uniform, jumped from his seat and held open the rear door.

"Kwati Umba, I come from the ministry. I have been chosen to escort you. It is a great honor."

Hayes looked the youthful soldier up and down. This was a representative of the new generation of FRELIMO warrior. What did they know of living like rats in the jungle, turned aside by villagers too frightened to feed them, hunted by mercenaries of the South African and Portuguese armies?

Nothing. But even the young in Mozambique knew their country had been born of blood.

The soldier took a note pad and pen from the pocket of his uniform. He was smiling bashfully.

"Kwati Umba, could I so disturb you to sign your name that I may show my village that I have met the Kwati Umba!" He looked down, embarrassed at the unsoldierly request.

Hayes chuckled and took the pen and pad. Kwati Umba was his African name, the name of the great general without a tribe who came from America to fight beside his black brothers in their struggle for liberation. Before that, and since, he had had other names. One was forgotten now by all but the FBI and several other law-enforcement agencies. The other, Claude Hayes, was the name that gave him membership in the most exclusive club in the world. He was a Soldier of Barrabas. One of the SOBs.

Hayes scribbled his African name on the paper and drew the head of a simba panther beneath it.

The soldier's face lit up with excitement. When Hayes handed the pad back, the young man held it as if it had magical powers.

"Let's go to the ministry now," Hayes suggested.

"Oh yes, Kwati Umba. We all await you with great pleasure!"

A moment later, the car was gliding through the broad ceremonial avenue that led into the government district. Hayes looked left and right, trying to absorb the familiar and the new. There was much of both. But something was missing, something he couldn't immediately put his finger on. When it occurred to him, he couldn't help chuckling.

"What happened to all the statues that used to line this street?" he asked the driver.

"All gone, Kwati Umba. We are a new country and had no use for those relics of our colonial history. The bronze statues of the Portuguese heroes were turned into bullets to help our brothers fight for the liberation of Zimbabwe."

"A good use for them."

The driver flashed a glance at Hayes in the rearview mirror. "From what is left, we make bullets to free our brothers in South Africa," the soldier said.

The car slowed in front of a long stone building built in the classical European style of the eighteenth century. They turned in a cobblestoned driveway that in turn led to a courtyard. An honor guard of tall black soldiers in the official green uniforms of the FRELIMO army snapped to attention as the car slid to a halt.

Hayes climbed out before the driver could get to his door, and the young man looked aghast, as if he had been derelict in his duty. Hayes smiled and waved his hand to signal that it didn't matter.

"Kwati Umba!"

He heard a deep voice boom out the name. An officer emerged from the high, carved entrance of the elegant ministry building. Gold braid glistened on his cuffs and epaulets, and silver medals and ribbons rattled on his chest.

The two men embraced, old soldiers and friends in greeting.

"What is all this, Simon Bituku?" Hayes waved to the soldiers standing stiffly at attention in two long rows across the courtyard.

"Did you think I would entertain my old commanding officer without impressing you with an honor guard?"

"But I came to see you as an old friend, Simon. Not as an official visitor."

"As a hero of the revolution, as one of the greatest fighters of the *chimurenga*, all your visits are official. Indeed, were it not for your stubborn refusal to accept the position of minister of defense after the war of liberation, you would be standing here in this uniform instead of me."

"It wasn't my style. I'm too much of a fighter to lead a peacetime army."

"So am I," Simon said mysteriously. He eyed the American. "Claude Hayes is the name you go by now?"

Hayes nodded. "A new life, a new name."

"How many is that now?"

"Three."

"Only three? In the villages and kraals where Kwati Umba is revered, it is said you have a hundred shapes, forms and names, that you change at will into bird or beast or man."

"And that the spirit M'Bando gave me this power in exchange for my promise to be an external warrior," Hayes continued, nodding his head.

"So you know the legends?"

Hayes nodded. "A worker at the hotel last night dropped the tray with my dinner on it. He was terrified, and when I made him explain he said he was afraid I would turn into a cheetah and tear him to pieces."

Both men laughed heartily.

"Come. I want to show you something." Simon Bituku, minister of defense in the Republic of Mozambique, and former officer in the guerrilla army led by Kwati Umba, motioned to the door. They climbed the steps and entered the long cool hallway of the building that had once housed the Portuguese colonial war office. Tall, black soldiers in uniform snapped to attention and saluted as they strode through the long dark corridors. When they approached the end of a distant wing of the ministry, Hayes could hear battle cries coming from outside.

"And are you still a warrior, Kwati Umba?"

"My name is Claude now, Simon."

Bituku nodded. "I shall respect that. Now that the *chimurenga* is over, we have different lives. More peaceful certainly, but sometimes some of us miss the battle, the years of struggle."

"Memory plays strange tricks," Hayes said thoughtfully. The two friends stood by the large double doors that led to another courtyard. "Somehow, as time goes by, it weeds out the bad things. The friends who got killed, the weeks of rain with no sleep and little food, our weapons rusting in our hands. Villages in flames and people slaughtered in ditches. Somehow those things end, and we remember instead the laughter we shared."

"We were brave and thought of nothing but the liberation of our country. Are you still a warrior?" Bituku repeated the question.

Hayes nodded. "I work for a guy in America. His name is...a secret. He's a good man, although he denies it. And he's the greatest fighter I've ever seen."

"Private work?"

Again Hayes nodded. Mercenary was a dirty word in this part of the world. "But we get to pick and choose our causes."

Simon Bituku smiled. "My government is working on a project now. Very secret. Perhaps you and I can participate for a few hours, for old times' sake. I, too, miss the fieldwork. But first, I want to show you this."

The minister pushed open a high wooden door. African heat pushed into the corridor, and feral battle cries slashed the calm air of the ministry. In a long grassy rectangle as large as a soccer field, and surrounded on all sides by wings of the defense ministry, two dozen boys and girls waited their instructor's command.

Both sexes were stripped to the waist, their black skins glistening and shiny with sweat, taut with muscles. Each youth held a short spear, and there was a target twenty yards away from them. One young man stood ahead of the others. His spear sailed in a graceful arc across the blue sky and hit the center of the target. Bull's-eye. The other young warriors broke into cheers. Walking tall and smiling with pride, the spear thrower returned to his rank.

A tall slim woman about sixteen took his place. She focused her concentration on the target and raised the spear in her right hand.

"Now every man and woman from the age of fourteen must learn to fight," Bituku said. "These are our most elite young warriors. They learn here, right inside the ministry, where the best teachers are available."

The young woman threw her spear, and again it hit the mark dead center.

"But spear throwing?" Hayes was surprised. "It was spears against rifles that made us lose this country a few hundred years ago."

"Their ability with modern arms will amaze you. But we also teach the traditional arts of war, that they might know their heritage. As you and I once learned it."

"True," said Hayes. "But we practiced spear throwing so we would not waste valuable ammunition."

"We learned the discipline because we needed to. They must learn discipline because they do not. If I recall—" Bituku faced Hayes with a look of challenge "—you and I were about the same in our skill. Come!"

Bituku introduced Kwati Umba to the young recruits. Their faces glowed with obvious surprise and reverence. Hayes scanned the two rows of new soldiers. After a ten-year absence, he was seeing in these proud faces the fruits of the long struggle he had waged as a guerrilla fighter.

Simon Bituku stripped off his uniform jacket and shirt and handed them to the instructor. Hayes noticed that his friend's body was still hard and muscled. Years at a desk job had not softened him a bit. On his shoulder, the tattoo of the simba panther remained, a symbol of Kwati Umba's army.

"Do you still have yours?" Bituku asked, following Hayes's glance as he gripped a spear in his right hand.

Hayes shook his head. "No, I had it removed. Sometimes it's better not to be easily identified."

Bituku held the spear back and drove it forward like a piston, flinging the shaft into the sky. It arced across the field and thudded into the target dead center.

"Bull's-eye!" Bituku exclaimed. The young soldiers burst into cheers and applause. "Can you beat that, old friend?"

Hayes stripped off his shirt. "What is this project you mentioned?" he asked as he reached for a spear.

"You must know that occasionally the South African army makes incursions into our country to kill guerrillas who operate against them."

Hayes nodded. "And your government allows it." He tossed the spear lightly in his hand to feel its weight.

"Of course," Bituku said. "South Africa is the last country in Africa in which the black man is still a slave. By day they are used as cheap labor in the mines and the dirty jobs of the cities. By night they are exiled to squalid townships or barren homelands. They have a right to their *chimurenga*, their war of freedom, just as we did. But tonight the project is a very simple one. Mine workers in the diamond fields smuggle diamonds to the guerrillas, who pass them to runners who bring them across the border to Mozambique. They are sold to finance the underground movement. Tonight these elite young soldiers will be taken to the border to observe the transfer. I invite you to come."

Hayes laughed. "In the United States we take kids to museums on class trips. Not battlefields."

"It's quite safe," Simon assured him. "Really."

Hayes raised the spear high over his shoulder. He narrowed his eyes and forced his concentration to the tip of the spearhandle already lodged in the target. The muscles of his back rippled with the powerful thrust of his arm.

The spear shot across the field, and the steel tip hit the butt of the spear Bituku had thrown, splitting it down the middle as Hayes's spear drove into the center of the target. The recruits burst into wild shouts of applause. One started yelling "Kwati Umba, Kwati Umba!" and the others quickly took up the chant.

Hayes faced them with a proud smile and his fist held high in salute. Simon Bituku laughed with pleasure at the welcoming.

"Will you come?" he urged.

Hayes did not miss the taunt in his old friend's eyes. He knew Barrabas and the American government that sponsored their covert-action team would not approve. But the temptation of Africa was too great.

"Sure," he said. "How can I refuse?"

WHEN MAJOR SNIDER walked back into his office in the security police headquarters in downtown Johannesburg, the prisoner was lying naked on the floor, half covered with a blanket. He was dead.

"We have the information you required, sir," Jacob, his young assistant, told him as he stepped over the corpse.

"Yes?" The major waited.

"The diamonds are smuggled across the border into Mozambique at a point near Punda Milla in Kruger

National Park. The exact location has been marked. Apparently, there is to be an exchange at ten o'clock tonight.''

"Excellent," Snider commented. He sat at his desk and pulled a sheaf of forms from the side drawer. "Anything else?"

"Yes. We managed to get the name of another cell member."

"The one who is smuggling the diamonds out of the mine?" Snider picked up a pen and looked at the form. It was an Accidental Death Report.

"Unfortunately not. He didn't know. But apparently this other cell member knows how the diamonds are smuggled out of the mine. His name is—" Jacob checked his notes "—Mthuli Sowanni."

Sidney Snider glanced quickly down the form, filling in the unfortunate prisoner's name and number. "Have him arrested," he said absently.

"It's being done now, sir."

"It's a secret I'm anxious to know, Jacob. The security at the diamond mines is extremely sophisticated. The only way they can smuggle diamonds out is with the assistance of someone in a very high position."

"I'm aware of that, sir."

"Someone white."

"Yes, sir."

"A traitor."

"Indeed."

"What do you suggest as cause of death, Jacob?"

"The usual, sir."

Major Snider wrote "Suicide" on the dotted line and signed the bottom.

3

The sunset threw a crimson flood over the Kalahari plains to the west of Johannesburg. The pace of the wealthy South African gold-mining metropolis slowed in the warm sweet breezes of evening that blew in from the high veldt. The streets among the canyons of skyscraping office towers emptied. In the residential neighborhood of Hillbrow, the sidewalks below the high-rise apartment buildings were crammed with pedestrians browsing in greengrocers or crowding into tiny cafés and bookstores.

And throughout the great city, the Bantu workers and domestics left their places of employment, their permits expired, and melted into the growing darkness that engulfed the black township of Soweto. The lights of Johannesburg gleamed like fire burning inside a diamond.

Johannesburg was white again.

Not far from the center of Johannesburg, just past the planetarium and the modern university of the Witwatersrand, shiny and expensive foreign cars turned off the De Villiers Graaf Motorway onto Jan Smuts Drive and headed for the wealthy suburb of Parktown. The license plate of a green Mercedes bore only four letters. BOSS. Bureau of State Security. It was a company car.

The Mercedes turned onto a tree-lined avenue and slowed before iron gates set in a high stone wall. The gates were brightly lit by mercury-arc lighting, and well-armed private guards stood at the entrance. They waved the black limousine ahead of the Mercedes through, and Snider eased his car forward until a man carrying a deadly looking Belgian FN-FAL stepped in front of him. Another man came to the window. Snider held up his papers without removing his mirrored sunglasses, and the guard nodded. Then Snider flipped his ID closed and tucked it inside the jacket of his tuxedo. The car eased forward through the gates.

He drove a few minutes up a slight incline and past long spacious lawns and gardens. The mansion came into view on a low bluff, which revealed all of Johannesburg sparkling under southern stars in the African night.

The drive was filled with cars, and every window of the great house was bright. The waltz music of Richard Strauss floated from the gardens. Men in black tie escorted women in ball gowns up the steps, where African servants held the great doors open. When Wilhelm Krudd celebrated Christmas, the elite of South Africa attended. As one of them, Major Snider was an important guest.

He left his car with a black attendant and walked briskly into the crowded foyer of the opulent mansion. A wide, carpeted stairway spiraled to the second floor, and a crystal chandelier hovered above the guests like a spaceship. Men in tuxes and women in jewels chitchatted. Black servants carried trays of brimming champagne glasses and elegant hors d'oeuvres among the crowd.

"Sidney!" A female voice crowed from across the room.

The man from BOSS turned to see a red-haired woman in a low-cut blue dress and a brilliant diamond necklace race across the room toward him. It was the wife of the minister of the interior. She had been on the make for him for some time, and Snider couldn't tell if she was a bored rich woman being mischievous or if her husband put her up to it to see how far the director of security could be lured into compromising himself. Such was the sensitive nature of his job.

"Sidney, so good to see you here," Vivienne gushed, pulling up to his side and pressing against him. "I'm so excited. We're all waiting for the surprise guest."

"Surprise guest?" the major said.

"Oh, do take off those sunglasses, Sidney. You don't need them here and they're so intimidating."

He pulled them from his eyes and folded them. Vivienne's diamonds almost blinded him. It wasn't just the necklace. She dripped diamonds. From earlobes, wrists, fingers and other places. He almost put his sunglasses back on.

"What surprise guest?" he repeated.

"You must have heard, Sidney. Willy promised us a surprise guest tonight. I'm so excited. I think it must be that famous movie star from Hollywood who's making a film in Cape Town right now."

"He couldn't possibly be a surprise," Snider replied. "He's standing over there in the doorway to the salon."

Vivienne's eyes grew large when she spotted the actor across the crowded room.

"I'm dying to talk to him."

"Please do," said Snider, backing away. These were normal people with normal concerns.

He felt a hand on his elbow, and turned to see Wilhelm Krudd's daughter, Sarah.

"Major Snider. My father would like to talk with you privately. He's in his study with some other gentlemen."

Snider tucked his sunglasses into his breast pocket and gazed at Sarah Krudd. "You are still the most beautiful woman in South Africa," he said with the beginning of a smile on his face.

Her short blond hair was the color of yellow straw in the bright sun, and glinted as if it was woven with gold. Her skin was smooth and soft, and her eyes sparkled like rare blue diamonds.

She blushed and laughed. "You're too gallant, Major Snider. You'll turn my head if I'm not careful. But thank you for the compliment."

"Where are your brothers?"

"Richard's in the study with father. Paul is..." She looked about the room to find him. She shrugged. "Who knows. You haven't met him yet, have you?"

"No. Even though he arrived from America months ago."

"You'll like him," Sarah assured Snider. "But he's quite different."

"Different?" The major's attention perked up at the mention of things different.

"Very relaxed and informal. I'm not sure if it's the influence of America, where he grew up, or the influence of our father's second wife, who raised him. We should hurry. My father's waiting."

She led him off through the foyer and into the crowded salon. Doors led out to a terrace where a small orchestra played waltzes. They continued deeper into the house, leaving the crowds and the sounds of the party behind them. Finally, they arrived at a paneled oak door.

"You must promise me one thing, Major Snider," Sarah said as she put her hand on his arm.

"Please call me Sidney, or Sid. My friends do." He closed his hand over hers. The one that a few hours earlier had been used as a weapon against an uncooperative prisoner now held Sarah's like a small white dove in the paw of a jackal.

She laughed slightly and drew her hand away as the door to the study opened. Wilhelm Krudd stood in front of them with a glass of Scotch in his hand. The older man smiled at the sight of his daughter and Major Snider.

"Sidney, come in! We've all been waiting for you." The rotund man was more jovial tonight than he had been at the Voortrekker Monument earlier that day.

"You wanted me to promise something?" Snider reminded Sarah.

"Only that whatever this business is you have to discuss, it will only take a few minutes. In case you haven't noticed, there's a party going on here tonight."

"My dear," Krudd said as he reached out and chucked his daughter's chin. "We all promise. No more than a few moments and we will be finished. Now let us alone, sweet one, and we can get to it."

Sarah smiled at Major Snider and her father. "I'll hold you to it," she warned humorously. "If you're not done shortly I'll come back in search of you."

"Twenty minutes at the most, my dear," her father assured her. Sarah left to join the party as Snider entered the wood-paneled study.

Krudd closed the door firmly behind him. The jokes were over and the party was now a world away. The atmosphere in this room was serious, and Krudd's other guests, who sat on the leather couches around the fireplace, looked grim.

"Have a seat, Major," Krudd invited him. "I suspect I need make no introductions."

Snider took the remaining chair and studied the faces of the other men with a quick scan.

Pieter van den Boos owned gold mines. The thin man clutched his drink with long spidery fingers. Along with Krudd, he provided financing for the projects they were about to discuss.

Next to him, an enormous fat man breathed heavily from the exertion of slurping back his Scotch and water. Horace Bloemvaal, the leading reverend of the Reformed Church in Pretoria, had a direct interest in this business. He was the head man of the big church for white people who supported the government's program of apartheid.

Next to him sat Henry Miller, the director of the Institute for Separate Development in Cape Town. Miller was a wimp. His shoulders sagged and his hands clutched his knees. His hair was greasy and thin, his smile nervous and timid. He was out of his league in this gathering. But as the director of an institute that developed theory for apartheid and lobbied for international acceptance of South Africa's racist laws, he had his contribution to make.

On the couch near Major Snider sat the last and newest member of the group. Richard Krudd was

Wilhelm's eldest son. He was not quite plump, but had a slightly overindulged look. Rolls of baby fat and the fact that he looked almost forty were both major accomplishments for a man who was at least fifteen years younger. Because he was heir to the vast Krudd diamond fortune, his father and South Africa had high expectations of him. He was eager to at least equal, if not surpass, them. So much so that once in a fit of pique he had almost beaten a black servant to death. It had taken some fast wheeling and dealing on Major Snider's part to hide the affair. Snider felt Richard Krudd was too hot and aggressive, potentially dangerous, to be a part of their little group. But Wilhelm insisted. And Wilhelm was the boss. Next, he supposed, the American son would be asked to join.

The diamond industrialist handed the director of state security a Scotch and water.

"Welcome, Major Snider, and all of you, to another meeting of the Inner Circle." He cleared his throat. It was time for a little speech.

"Our country, it is apparent, is in crisis." He paced in front of the fireplace slowly as he talked. "The twenty-two million blacks living in the townships outside the cities are restless, and riots are becoming more frequent. Liberal American politicians visit and stir up trouble, and on the northern border, the former colonies of Rhodesia and Mozambique now have black majority governments. The border zone is like a sieve, with guerrillas and saboteurs crossing almost at will. And to top it off, a bunch of churches have elected a black man to become bishop of Johannesburg. Soon, if things are not stopped, America will begin economic sanctions against us. That is why we have formed the Inner Circle."

"Indeed, that's our purpose," Horace Bloemvaal said in an oily nasal voice. "To destroy Bishop Toto, and through him, the black opposition once and for all."

"Major Snider!" Krudd addressed the man from BOSS. "We've asked you here tonight for a report on the Bishop Toto plot."

Snider crossed his legs and gave his audience a satisfied smile. "Gentlemen, all has gone according to plan. The impostor has been given full instructions, and he will be completely cooperative. At the appropriate time, the real Bishop Toto will be removed and secretly imprisoned. The impostor will take his place. We will conduct a disinformation campaign to make it appear that Bishop Toto is willing to make great concessions to the white government. This will alienate and enrage his followers. On the day of his consecration in Johannesburg, two weeks from now, he will make a speech calling for the dismemberment of Black nationalist organizations and full cooperation with the system of apartheid. His followers will see this as a complete betrayal, which of course it is, and at the time my people can guarantee a riot. In the riot, Bishop Toto will unfortunately be killed by his own people. Or by us."

"And the entire African opposition to our government will be discredited in the eyes of the world," Henry Miller enthused. "It's brilliant."

"If it works," Pieter van den Boos said grumpily.

"Of course it will work," Bloemvaal insisted. "God has ordained it. The victory of our people at Blood River..."

"Yes, yes. Not all of us take the Voortrekkers mystique so seriously, however."

"I do, Mr. van den Boos," Snider stated, clearly annoyed.

"Yes. Your periodic visits to that mausoleum on the Pretorian Hill are a well-known eccentricity, Major Snider."

"It is a site of tremendous importance to us." Snider's words were chilly with outrage.

"Perhaps," van den Boos said impatiently. "I'm merely concerned about my business interests."

"Gentlemen," said Wilhelm Krudd, leaping in to soothe the ruffled feelings of the Inner Circle. "I can assure you that the impostor is perfect. Staggering really. Through Major Snider, I saw him today. I personally guarantee the accuracy of what the major has told us."

"Then where is he hidden?" van den Boos asked.

Snider responded quickly. "For security reasons, I think it best that only I and Wilhelm Krudd know."

The rotund Bloemvaal pouted. "You think we can't be trusted, Major?"

"I..." Sidney began. Van den Boos interrupted.

"On the other hand, if only Sidney knows, only Sidney can be held responsible for any mishaps."

"There won't be any," Snider emphasized. "Everything will go according to plan."

"Except for some further information my father has." Richard Krudd finally spoke. His lips were curled in a slight sneer, as if the man from BOSS were slightly inferior. "Information that will undoubtedly complicate the situation."

Snider looked at Krudd, alarmed. Their host cleared his throat nervously and set his Scotch on the mantel. "It's not as serious as all that, gentlemen. Really just some information that happened to come my way from our friend the minister of foreign affairs. Apparently the American government, under pressure from certain liberal senators, no doubt, is concerned about potential assassination plots against Bishop Toto. They are particularly concerned that someone might try to take a potshot at him when he makes his speech outside the cathedral.''

''And why should that be of concern to us?'' Van den Boos became increasingly querulous. ''If our plans go ahead without problems, Bishop Toto will die and white South Africa will not be in the least to blame.''

''Quite so,'' Krudd said nervously. ''Nevertheless, they have been putting pressure on our government. In consultation with the minister, I took the liberty of suggesting that the American government send its own covert-action team to guard against Toto's assassination.''

Expressions of surprise and shock went around the room. Only Snider remained unmoved.

''Do you really think that a good idea?'' the director of the institute asked. ''What if they find out?''

''Gentlemen, it's a token concession. The American team will simply go over the security arrangements before the consecration and accompany some of our people on the day of the ceremonies. Major Snider can easily see to it that they do not get in the way.''

''It's perfect!'' Snider glowed with satisfaction as he confronted his fellow conspirators with his enthusiasm. ''Ha! The American team will verify that we did everything we could to protect the bishop. Then they'll see his own people kill him! Not only that, but the arrival of the Americans will present us with the perfect opportunity to make the switch."

Van den Boos let out a scratchy laugh. "Then let the Americans send who they will," he said as the laughter became a short hacking cough. "Major Snider, despite my initial doubts, I am beginning to have confidence in your—"

Suddenly, a small red light at the base of the clock on the mantel began to glow. Electronic sensors outside the room had detected the presence of someone at the door.

Wilhelm Krudd jumped from the chesterfield and opened it.

"Hellooooo!" The boisterous voice of the person outside had a distinctly American accent. A handsome, dark-haired young man in his early twenties walked into the room with a big smile and burst into a chorus of song.

"I'm dreeaming of a whiiiite Christmaas..." He stopped when no one laughed. Or smiled. "You're all so serious! Champagne anyone?" The young man held up a half-empty bottle.

"Gentlemen." Wilhelm Krudd turned to face his colleagues of the Inner Circle. "My youngest son, Paul. He has just returned from America to his homeland."

"And loves it!" Paul cried with enthusiasm. "Gentlemen, the pleasure is mine." He gave them a deep, exaggerated bow.

"You set off the sensors, Paul!" His older brother Richard chastised him, pointing to the little flashing light on the mantel.

"The sensors?" Paul said in mock astonishment. "Now why on earth would there be sensors?"

"Servants have a tendency to eavesdrop," Richard Krudd explained hastily.

"Industrial espionage is a serious problem," Snider added. He pushed himself up from the chesterfield. "Were you outside the door long?" he asked, his eyes narrowing.

"What! Me eavesdrop? L'il ol' me!" Paul faked an accent from the American Deep South, and blinked his eyes in complete innocence.

"Oh, nonsense, Sidney," Wilhelm Krudd broke in, laughing at the joke. He put his arm around his son and explained. "Sidney is the director of state security and a very suspicious man. That's what he's paid for. He's very good at his job, too, so we must indulge him, even if sometimes he appears to be a little overdedicated."

"Well, gentlemen," Paul said with a wide smile, "Sarah sent me here with strict instructions to lead you out into the wonderful world of Christmas parties. Besides, your special guest has arrived, father, and you are required to meet him. His appearance certainly has caused quite a sensation. They almost choked on their champagne when he came in the door, so I had the servants crack open a few more cases to help them steel their nerves."

Paul opened the door and started to leave. "In any event, I know you're doing your own thing here, so I'll leave you with Sarah's notice and you can risk her wrath yourselves. Gentlemen." He bowed theatrically again and left the room.

"Doing our own thing," Bloemvaal muttered distastefully.

Wilhelm Krudd shook his head. "His mother, my second wife, raised him in the U.S.A. Over my objections, I might add. He's odd in some ways, but he does seem to be adjusting to life in South Africa quite well.''

Major Snider stared silently at the door Paul had closed behind him as if his vision passed through the wood and followed the young man back to the party.

"Well then," Wilhelm Krudd said, rubbing his hands quickly. "The meeting's adjourned. Shall we join the others?"

The Inner Circle left the study with Wilhelm Krudd and Major Snider walking slowly behind. The hubbub of voices and the clink of champagne glasses grew louder as they passed through several rooms toward the foyer and salon.

"Paul's political ideas," Snider asked, "are they racially secure?"

"Tsk, tsk, Sidney. Your suspicions are working overtime. Like most Americans, Paul doesn't seem to have any. At first our policy of apartheid seemed very odd to him, but he's adjusting marvelously. He loves his work at the diamond mines. He's in the office, of course, and I'm sure in a few years he'll join his older brother, Richard, on the board."

In the salon, a large party of revelers crowded around the Christmas tree. Krudd had to stand slightly on his toes to see over the heads and shoulders of his guests.

The special guest was entertaining extraordinarily well. The short, middle-aged man in a clerical collar spoke in a pleasant high-pitched voice and smiled frequently. He had warm brown eyes and a gentle manner. Like the servants, his skin was black.

Snider glanced at the faces of the wealthy guests who had gathered around to listen to the famous Bishop Toto. The real one.

Most of them looked puzzled or ill at ease. Events in the outside world were forcing them to take stock of the Africans who shared their country. Nonetheless, the only blacks they, like most white South Africans, ever spoke to were their servants. It was most difficult for them to relate to a black who was both an intellectual and a political leader.

For a moment Major Snider felt the blind rage from the afternoon session flooding through his body. His hands tightened, pulling at the raw skin on his knuckles. He certainly knew how to relate to blacks.

"Willy! Sidney!" Vivienne, the red-haired, diamond-studded wife of the government minister ran toward them. "What a surprise," she gushed. "Bishop Toto at your party. I don't know what to say!"

"Vivienne, my dear. It's important that the dialogue between whites and blacks in our country grow," Krudd told her. "Bishop Toto agreed to make an appearance to show he's sincere in reaching out to everyone."

"Oh, Willy. You're the savior of our country. You really are."

Krudd and Snider exchanged knowing glances.

"Thank you, my dear. Now why don't you go and talk to the bishop."

"Talk?" Vivienne looked completely at a loss. "But what would I have to say to him?"

"Talk about Christmas," Major Snider suggested gently. "He's a bishop."

"Oh, what a good idea, Sidney." Vivienne disappeared back into the crowd.

"It's astonishing," Krudd murmured to the man from BOSS. "Seeing the real Bishop Toto tonight only confirms what I saw earlier today. The impostor is perfect!"

The two men backed away from the crowd and walked to the terrace where they could speak privately. The orchestra had switched from Strauss waltzes to Christmas songs, and the strains of Paul's earlier tune drifted through the mansion. A young woman earnestly crooned "...of a whiiite Christmaas..."

"What will we do to Toto once we have made the substitution?" Krudd asked.

"We'll keep him for a few days as an insurance policy," Snider said. "Then we'll kill him. Oh, by the way..." He glanced quickly at his watch. It was almost ten o'clock.

"Concerning those raw diamonds that are being stolen from your mines. An informer revealed the border area where they are taken across to Mozambique. There is to be an exchange tonight apparently."

"Ah, excellent. Finally you have made progress in that matter. You have been busy lately, Major. So what is being done about it?"

"The South African air force and army will attack the guerrilla positions inside Mozambique."

"Excellent! When?"

Major Sidney looked at his watch again. "In about ten minutes."

Wilhelm Krudd raised his champagne glass and clinked it against the major's. "Merry Christmas, Sidney."

"Merry Christmas," Snider replied.

4

Claude Hayes gazed out over the high rolling hills that descended to the savannas of northeastern South Africa. The border was a few miles away. Warm breezes blew in from the veldt, and the sky was bright with stars. The gaunt spindly shadows of baobab trees stood dark on the crest of the hill. Their giant water-bloated trunks towered over the dry thorn brushes and mopane trees, which ended in their headdresses of spindly twig branches.

The mercenary walked back to the encampment. The young warriors from the elite training class squatted on the dry grass while Simon Bituku and his aides paced and spoke softly together.

The guerrilla contacts from South Africa were almost an hour late, and the Mozambique officials debated a course of action.

Simon turned to Hayes. "We discuss if we should send out a party to scout along the border. It's very dangerous. There are always South African patrols and sometimes they do not stay on their side of the frontier."

Hayes nodded, and without replying walked back to the crest of the hill to gaze out over his beloved Africa. His ears strained through the noises of the night, sifting out insects, the rustle of vegetation in the soft breezes, far away the occasional satisfied growl of a well-fed lion and the screech of monkeys fleeing to the safety of their tree roosts.

Simon had given him an AK-47, the standard rifle of the Mozambique armed forces, as it was of guerrilla forces throughout the world. The AK was primitive but extremely effective. Its simplicity as an automatic rifle made certain it didn't often malfunction in the field. Unlike the American M-16 it was highly resistant to dust and water. That was an important consideration when it came to battle operations of the hit-and-run kind, far from military supply lines.

He slipped the Russian assault rifle off his shoulder and fingered the distinctive 30-round curved magazine that extended just below the barrel in front of the trigger. He had long since come to prefer the M-16 for its lightness and firepower, and it had been years since he had held his old friend Kalashnikov.

Restless and tired of waiting, Hayes gripped the AK in his hand and walked down the hill toward the clump of mixed aloe and euphorbia bushes at the bottom. Twenty yards from the copse, the sudden flapping of wings gave away the flight of a screech of giant bats from the spindly top of another baobab tree.

Hayes stopped.

He listened very carefully to the noises of the night.

Someone was breathing. Very faintly, but not far away.

He raised his rifle and walked to a clump of thorny shrubs. His feet scratched at the dry, gravelly soil. The breathing stopped.

Hayes crouched low behind a clump of euphorbia bushes and continued to move forward in a silent duck walk until he came to the trunk of the aloe tree. He could hear the breathing again, long and slow but with a jagged edge to it. Someone was trying to remain concealed.

He stood and stepped forward into the copse, the AK steel tight against his hands and his tendons coiled to spring.

He swung quickly around the aloe and stood face-to-face with a terrified African. The man tried to make a run for it, but he stumbled and fell, clutching his stomach. His clothing was wet with blood.

He tried to scramble away from the merc on his hands and knees, but Hayes ran to his side, calling softly in Swahili, "Do not be afraid. I will help you."

He laid his gun down and leaned over the supine body. The man stared up at him, the whites of his eyes bulging from his face. His features indicated he was of Xhosa origin. As Hayes peeled away the bloody shirt and saw the wound, the man's breath came in short painful jerks.

A knife or bayonet had pierced his stomach and opened up the bowels. Dark blood frothed from the long wound. He was dying. There was nothing anyone could do this far away from a major hospital.

"You are from the Spear of the Nation," Hayes said, calling the South African guerrilla organization by its name. "I am with Simon Bituku. From Maputo."

The man nodded. He swallowed to clear his throat, and Hayes paused, for a moment uncertain what to do. He did not want to leave the man here to die.

"They have found us. My companions are dead. I escaped," the dying African said painfully.

"The South African army?"

The guerrilla nodded. Hayes felt him press a small leather pouch into his hand.

"Here are the diamonds." The man coughed and blood spilled from his mouth. He began to choke.

"Don't talk," Hayes told him. "I'll carry you up the hill to safety."

The dying guerrilla shook his head regretfully. He grabbed Hayes's sleeve and clenched it tight in his fist. "There is a diamond hidden in the mine that is the biggest diamond ever discovered." His eyes filled suddenly with peacefulness and looked somewhere far away. "It is the new Star of Africa. Yes! The New Star!" His weakening voice became wondrous. His hand on Hayes's shirt gripped tighter, and pulled him closer. "It is hidden in the mine," he said urgently, with sudden strength. "We were ready to move it but—" the man coughed blood again, and Hayes felt his grip weaken "—there...there is an informer." Bright frothy blood spilled down his chin and onto his chest.

Far to the west, Hayes heard the distant drone. Airplanes. Bombers. And they were coming fast.

"Who is the contact in the mine?" he asked, racing the words.

The man muttered something, faintly, fighting against his closing eyes. He tried to speak, but stopped abruptly. For a second he froze. Then his head fell back and life left his body. His eyes did not close.

Hayes pried the dead man's hand from his sleeve. The skin on the back of it was rough and hard. Embedded under the flesh with charcoal powder was the tattoo of the head of the panther.

As the sound of the airplanes grew louder, Hayes grabbed the little leather pouch and ran for the encampment, half a mile away. Out of the western sky the darkened outlines of the three jets were visible like thin deadly needles.

He yelled to warn Simon and the others of the danger, but had barely covered a quarter of the distance to the camp when the war planes threw their first rockets.

The crest of the hill erupted in an orange explosion, showering earth and bits of baobab tree down on Hayes. The concussion waves banged against him like the cuff of a mighty hand, throwing him backward.

The force of the explosion drove him to the brink of unconsciousness as he rolled down the hill. He stopped his fall and pushed the ground to get up.

The airplanes launched three more rockets, and one after the other the rockets raced their red tracers to impact. The hillside and ground erupted in flames, and again the concussion waves rolled back like a steel tire, deafening him and throwing him carelessly down like a weightless stickman. His vision went black, specked by exploding pinpricks of color. His consciousness was reduced to a tiny voice far in the back of his mind. It ordered him to get up.

As he did, he saw the three jets, shadows of death dark against the stars of the African night, grow small in the distance.

The still had returned to bushveldt, but on the ridge of the hill, trees and grass burned in a long line. The roar of the fire was like a fiendish cackling. The devil's mirth.

He ran, the air beating inside his chest and the blood pounding into his head. He heard himself yelling one word over and over again. Simon. There was no answer.

He stood at the crest of the hill, amid the crackle of the fires. The acrid smoke stung his eyes. The heat of the flames burned against his skin. He walked through the torn earth looking for his friends.

They were gone.

A final explosion startled him. One of their jeeps blew into fragments as the gas tank caught. The other vehicles were already burning balls of unrecognizably twisted metal.

The smoke carried the unmistakable sweet odor of burning flesh. He saw them, spread across the soil of the homeland, twisted and charred bodies and bits of bodies. His companions. This was the land they protected, defended, fought for and finally died for.

Now they were a part of it.

Tears welled in his eyes, easing the irritation from the smoke. But the crying came from the sorrow that ran through his body like a wild river let loose by a broken dam.

The light leather pouch was still in his hand. He tugged the strings at the top of it and poured the contents into his palm. A king's ransom in uncut diamonds lay there. The raw stones, like soapy glass, were worthless compared to what had just been snuffed out.

Claude Hayes turned and looked down from the Mozambique hill to the land that rolled down the veldts of South Africa.

He had already fought a war for the liberation of some of his African brothers. But that war wasn't over yet. And whether he would continue to fight didn't require a decision; the decision had been made by the color of his skin.

His nostrils flared. One hand tightened around the precious stones, the other around his AK-47. The border into South Africa was two miles to the west.

He started down the hill in that direction.

5

A week later and a world away, Nile Barrabas
stretched his long, muscled frame across the mat-
tress, lost somewhere between sleep and dreaming. His
right arm and leg automatically reached sideways toward Erika. When they encountered nothing, he felt
around. The other half of the bed was empty. He
sniffed. The smell of coffee drifted in from the living
room of the hotel suite. Erika was already having
breakfast. He opened his eyes and looked out the
window. The December sky was crisp and blue over
Central Park. It was a beautiful day. For a thousand
dollars a night, the weather was included in the bill.

The door opened quietly and Erika stepped noiselessly into the room. She glanced at him quickly.

"You're awake." It wasn't a question.

"Yeah."

She walked to the closet to look for something in her
suitcase.

"Hey, listen, I'm sorry about last night," he said as
he sat up and propped himself against the pillows.

She didn't answer. She just kept sorting through her
clothing, pulling out a blouse and holding it up to her
chest. She found the one she wanted and pulled the T-
shirt she was wearing over her head. Her long blond
hair cascaded down over her smooth white shoulders,
framing her breasts.

"I'm really sorry," Barrabas repeated.

"Oh, Nile." Finally she looked up at him, shaking her hair back and standing with her hands on her hips.

"We've known each other for years. Off and on. I know what it's like for you when you have to work." She put her arms through the sleeves of a white silk blouse and lowered it over her head. It slipped smoothly down her long arms, the delicate white cloth coming to a rest on her slender shoulders. The neckline fell slightly, revealing a hint of cleavage. She walked to the full-size mirror, tucking the blouse into her jeans. "It's just that..." She trailed off, looking at herself in the mirror. Barrabas could tell she was choosing her words carefully.

"It's fine for you," she said finally, adjusting the folds of the silk at her thin waist. "Every time they give you another war to fight, you just go off and fight it."

"But I seem to need it, Erika. I need to live that way. Besides, it's the only kind of work I know." He said the last part with a smile, but as she looked at him she didn't smile back.

"And you always have me to come home to. Waiting for you in Amsterdam or Paris or New York. How do you think it feels for me?" She turned from the mirror to face him. "One minute we're enjoying ourselves, the next you're flying off to some goddamn spot and all I have to do is sit around and wait to hear if you're..."

She faltered, and she didn't finish the sentence. She tightened her belt.

"If I'm dead or not," Barrabas supplied.

She didn't look at him.

"That's what you were going to say, isn't it?"

"I'm tired of putting my life on hold every time you get a phone call. It's Christmas in ten days, Nile. And Jessup's been trying to get hold of you again. What am I supposed to do?"

Barrabas threw back the covers and swung himself around so he was sitting on the edge of the bed, facing her.

"So this time I'll tell Jessup to take his job somewhere else."

"You tried that the last time."

Nile Barrabas was at a loss for words. His head dropped, and he contemplated the carpet while he thought of something right to say. His left thigh still had a livid scar where a bullet had pierced it a few months earlier. Erika was right. The last time he'd said no was when the Fixer had asked him to eliminate a torture master who was imprisoned in a Cuban fortress. As it turned out, other events pulled him into the adventure against his will.

Tony Lopez, the kid brother of a mercenary who had worked and died for Barrabas, had run off to join his dead brother's buddies. Instead, he managed to get entangled in a plot by a terrorist group called X Command to liberate the torturer. Tony Lopez was the bait, X Command was the lure and Nile Barrabas and his soldiers, the SOBs, were the prey. They had been targeted for elimination by a connection in Washington they were still trying to uncover.

That job put three of his men, Liam O'Toole, Billy Starfoot and Nate Beck, temporarily out of commission with bullet or knife wounds and left him with the sore leg.

Erika got the raw end of the deal, because he'd had to interrupt a vacation with her then. But it was hard for Barrabas to figure out another way of doing it. It wasn't just the fact that leading a group of mercenaries on covert-action assignments *was* about the only kind of work he knew how to do. When he got right down to it, it was the only thing he *wanted* to do.

"You know I get restless," he told her.

"What do you think I get when you're away?" Erika answered. She leaned her back against the window and the view of Central Park and folded her arms across her chest. She looked him dead in the eye. "That's the whole point, Nile. You need your jobs. I'm not enough for you. And it pisses me off."

She turned abruptly and looked out the window. She was sulking.

"I'll tell Jessup no this time. It's Christmas. Let's spend it somewhere alone. We can go to Wyoming. We can stay on the run, just the two of us. The rest of the world can rotate without us."

He stood up and walked to the slender blond Dutch woman, standing behind her and clasping her in his strong arms. He felt her leaning her small body against his, the soft curves bending into the hard tautness of his own. "I love you," he said.

"Promise?"

"Yeah," he said, rubbing his face in her hair. "I promise."

TED'S BAR AND LOUNGE was tucked away on Forty-sixth Street, not far from Times Square. By the time Barrabas got there on foot from the hotel, he could feel his left thigh tingling with a little fatigue. The bullet wound had healed quickly, but the muscle was still rebuilding its strength. A Christmas vacation with Erika would give him time to get that strength back.

He stopped when he saw Ted's sign overhead. Everything going on between Erika and him suddenly hit him. He understood her feelings. But passing up a job and hanging around New York or going to Wyoming would be like having time on his hands. It was the best way to kill a relationship he could think of. Erika knew that as well as he did. She wasn't asking him any favors this morning. She was telling him it was over.

He steeled himself. He was going to have to play this one by ear. Jessup first.

Barrabas wheeled through the glass door into the warm, steamy lounge.

Ted's was a quiet unobtrusive place where ordinary Americans came to sit at the bar and tell the bartender their troubles, or line up at the open kitchen where the short-order cook with tattoos dished out the day's specials of overboiled vegetables and corned beef.

Barrabas spotted the Fixer immediately, back in the far corner digging into a $2.95 Big Pig Special. Choosing restaurants was a game he and the Fixer liked to play. For every elegant affair Jessup forced Barrabas to endure, Barrabas picked out something scuzzy to inflict on Jessup. Invariably, however, the enormous man was undeterred and whatever food was available, he ate.

The ex-CIA agent's vast bulk betrayed that secret. Barrabas shook his head and swore one thing he'd already sworn a hundred times before. He'd rather a brief encounter with a bullet and a one-way trip to nowhere before he let himself go to pot like that.

Everyone made his choices. After ten years in the U.S. Army and a brief slice of heroism in Vietnam, Nile Barrabas made his. He was a soldier. Very professional, very businesslike, a lot of expertise and a reputation as the hand of death. He liked his life best when he put it on the line.

Jessup was waving him over.

The tall mercenary with the distinctive short-clipped white hair and green eyes in a face hardened more by war than by age, walked down the long bar. He nodded to Ted, who wiped the counter with a dirty cloth.

"I see you ordered the house specialty," Barrabas commented. "Congratulations."

"My eye for food is more discriminating than your eye for restaurants, fortunately. Actually it's not bad."

He plunged another heavy forkful of pork-loin roast into his mouth and chewed. His eyes did not look up to meet Barrabas's.

"What's wrong, Jessup?" The white-haired warrior knew how to read the signs of bad news.

Before the Fixer could answer, a nearby door leading to the rest rooms opened and a tall woman with short brown hair stepped out. Barrabas was surprised. It was Lee Hatton. Jessup swallowed quickly.

"I was just about to tell you, Nile."

"Tell him what?" the woman said as she pulled her chair back and sat. Barrabas noticed a half-filled glass of beer at her place that he'd missed when he sat down. But he picked up on a few other things almost immediately. Her voice was tense and her eyes were red.

She started rummaging through the shoulder bag she carried.

"That you were in Washington and came up to New York with me."

Lee nodded. "I was visiting some old friends," she said. "Since our Russian friends blew up Casa Hatton, I've been living out of a suitcase and relying on the hospitality of acquaintances. So was..." It was a moment of failure. She closed her shoulder bag and leaned her face into her hand.

"What's happened?" Barrabas asked softly.

Jessup looked at him but paused before answering.

"Claude," said Hatton. "We've both been traveling since the house on Majorca was destroyed. He didn't have a place to call home, either. He went to Mozambique to visit some old friends of his in FRELIMO."

Jessup silently took a news clipping from the file beside him and laid it on the table in front of Barrabas. An incursion by South African bombers into Mozambique had wiped out a terrorist stronghold.

"It happened a week ago," said Jessup. "Yesterday the authorities in Maputo released the names of the dead. Their minister of defense, Simon Bituku, was one of them. And a hero from their war of liberation named Kwati Umba."

Jessup didn't have to say more. Claude Hayes's African name was known to them all.

"No!" Barrabas said, denying what the newspaper clipping made clear.

"Apparently Hayes and Bituku went to the border zone to inspect some kind of guerrilla exfiltration setup. In the meantime, the South Africans found themselves an informer and attacked. The Mozambique government declared a state of national alert and a month of mourning."

"Two more martyrs for the wars," Barrabas muttered as he pushed the clipping back to Jessup. The Fixer pushed aside his food. He leaned forward with both hands flat on the table.

"Which brings me to my next point, Nile."

"A job."

Jessup inclined his head a fraction in what passed for a nod. "Sort of." His eyes went from conspiratorial to devious.

"Look, Jessup. Either it's a job or it isn't. Just like my answer will either be yes or no."

Lee Hatton spoke up. "What he means, Nile, is that there's no official authorization for this one."

"That's right. Some people in Washington came to me. People who sit on the same house committee as the senator."

Barrabas's lip curled at the mention of the politician. The last job he'd been on, the Cuban caper, had been a setup. And he had plenty of reason to believe the senator and some of his cohorts had been behind it.

Jessup continued. "They tried to get the project approved for covert action, but the majority on the committee wouldn't go for it."

"And the senator controls the majority."

Jessup nodded. "So they want it done, anyway."

"My fees?" Barrabas asked. It was usually six figures. At least.

Jessup coughed delicately. "Well, that's a problem."

"Since they can't get committee approval, there are no funds to pay a covert-action team," Lee told him.

"Hold it right there!" Barrabas faced both of them squarely across the table with his hands held up in front of him. "I know where both of you are going on this one. Forget it. Charity may begin at home, but I already gave at the office."

"Oh, shit, Colonel!" Hatton reacted with uncharacteristically intense anger. "You're about the finest fighting machine this side of the Atlantic. And you're already a rich man, so you don't do it for the money. Alex Nanos and Geoff Bishop and I are ready to go and we'll go with or without you!"

Barrabas looked at Jessup as the setup dawned. Now he knew why Hatton was here. Jessup the Fixer was fixing it so he wouldn't back out of whatever was coming.

"What's the scoop?" he asked grimly.

"You've probably heard of Bishop Toto, the black leader who's just been elected bishop of Johannesburg. Our people feel he's our only hope for a voice of moderation in South Africa. The radical whites want to keep the Africans as cheap labor."

"Or slaves."

"By any other name, yes. And the radical blacks, not without some justification, want to drive the whites into the sea. Our information is that there's an assassination conspiracy underway against Bishop Toto."

"Who's behind it?"

Jessup shrugged. "Our information comes from independent informers who are linked into the American intelligence network. The evidence suggests the suspects to be fanatical extremist whites. But let's face it, it could just as well be the blacks."

"Especially after what's been going on in the past week," Hatton added.

"What's that?"

"Toto made a guest appearance at the home of a prominent white South African. He alienated some of his more extremist followers, and they're accusing him of compromise now that he's been elected bishop."

"And what does Toto say?"

"That it's important for him to use his position to influence people, even if that means entering the camp of the enemy," Hatton concluded.

Jessup interjected. "Toto is going to be consecrated next week at the cathedral in Johannesburg.

The tensions between the black people and the white rulers of South Africa are high. They're even higher now because of Bishop Toto's recent statements. His consecration could turn into an ugly riot.''

"So what are the SOBs supposed to do about it?''

"Not much, actually,'' Hatton said, staring into her draft beer. "But I'm going to do it for Claude. It was a cause he fought for and believed in. And I figure actions speak louder than words.''

Barrabas looked at the sole woman warrior on his team and waited for her to finish.

"I mean,'' she said, "when someone dies, it's fine to say you're sorry and cry all the tears you want. But it's not good enough for me. I get angry. I want to fight.''

"So what's the job?'' Barrabas asked Jessup.

"You go into South Africa. Lee has some connections to the wealthy Krudd diamond family. You'll meet lots of people. You keep your eyes open. Through the Krudd family connection you'll be given carte blanche to do what you want, go where you want, talk to whoever you want. And if all goes well you'll be home for Christmas.''

"Sounds like we're not supposed to get our hands dirty,'' Barrabas commented, glancing from Jessup to Hatton.

"The South Africans have given us permission to send a team to observe the security arrangements around Bishop Toto. That's your cover,'' Jessup told him.

"What we do on our own time,'' Lee said with a smile, "is up to us.''

"Like find any would-be assassins and remove them from the picture?''

Lee nodded. Jessup stared and waited for an answer from the colonel.

Barrabas reached into his shirt pocket and pulled out a cigar. "South Africa's very dangerous," he mused, biting off the end and licking the cigar. "It's a police state. The secret police there were trained by Nazis after the war." He struck a match and lit the cigar slowly until the end glowed. He blew out a long funnel of smoke over their heads. Hatton and Jessup couldn't tell if he was thinking it out, or just making them wait. Barrabas was doing both.

"Okay," he said. "When do we leave?"

It was later, when he was outside making his way back through the slush-filled street to Times Square that he thought of Erika. He plunged his hands deep into the pockets of his sheepskin jacket, and clenched the stub of his cigar between his teeth.

"Oh, shit," he groaned, remembering his promise to her.

Even before he fished a quarter out of his pocket to make the phone call, he indexed in his mind a list of excuses. Then he chucked the list into his mental garbage pile of dumb and dishonest things.

Putting a challenge in front of him, as Jessup and Hatton had just done in Ted's Lounge, was like laying a syringe in front of a junkie. There was no way he could refuse.

Erika already knew that.

He stepped into a phone booth and plugged the quarter in the slot. The hotel switchboard connected him to the suite. The phone rang. There was no answer until the operator came back on the line.

Erika had already checked out.

6

More than a million people lived in Soweto, making it
one of the largest townships in Africa. Yet it was
found on few maps. It took its name from the *south
west to*wnships outside Johannesburg. It was an immense ghetto, which supplied the city and the gold
mines with an enormous reservoir of cheap African
labor.

The sprawling city had no cultural center and no
downtown. Miles of shabby brick houses with corrugated iron roofs lined the rutted roads shoulder to
shoulder. Sometimes these were mixed with one-story
school buildings, little churches or small storefronts.
But for the most part, the seedy streets revealed a
continuous monotony.

Claude Hayes was a weary dusty traveler when he
rolled into Soweto. He avoided the security police at
the gates across the road leading into the townships by
entering on foot across open fields and through
backyards.

He trudged slowly past the houses and little stores
with bins of produce and bolts of cloth under awn-
ings out in front. Ancient pickup trucks rattled past,
carrying loads of melons and yams, and children
chanted in an old school bus that creaked by. Pariah
dogs contested for the loudest bark in the dusty streets,

and women in colorful native dress and turbans held little children with stoical brown eyes.

Hayes searched the doorways along the street for the sign he had been told to look for. He had crossed into South Africa a week earlier, the night of the ambush in Mozambique. It took him a day to cover the fifty-mile overland distance to the Vanda Bantustan, a homeland or reservation for Africans in the north-eastern corner of the country. Like most of the other African homelands, which had been granted to the black population by the government, Vanda perched on arid, infertile mountain peaks just south of the Limpopo River. The people were poor and hungry. Nothing grew there. There was no work. And without permits they could not leave to seek jobs in the city.

In a settlement, he had found a school, and at the school students who, like the students of Mozambique ten years earlier, studied revolution. He told them he was an American traveling in Africa, and like all good revolutionaries, they did not ask questions. They soon listened to the spaces between the words of his story, and knew that somewhere, somehow, in one of the many wars that raged across their continent, Claude Hayes had been active.

They fed him and directed him into the underground network that smuggled Africans from the homelands to the cities.

Four days after he arrived in Vanda, Hayes found himself riding in a melon truck two hundred miles to a second Bantustan called Bophuthatswana. He rested there another day and a half before traveling the last fifty miles to Soweto on foot.

More than anything else, he needed identification papers and a travel permit. With those, he could venture outside the homelands without being harassed and imprisoned by white authorities. With papers he could get a job at the diamond mines. He could avenge the death of Simon Bituku.

His eyes scanned the fronts of the little stores and houses on the Soweto street, looking for the sign the students had told him about. Finally he saw it. Three zigzag lines in black, red and yellow. This was where he had to stop.

The buildilng was a store with a rickety wooden veranda running along the front. The windows were dark in the shadow of the eaves, and an old man, wrinkled by time and wind, rocked on the porch, his eyes closed. A swarm of flies buzzed sadistically around his head.

Hayes went up two steps onto the wooden porch and plunged through the doors.

The room inside was much bigger than it looked from the street. It was the size of a small supermarket, with sawdust-covered wooden floors. There were six pool tables, a long bar and a few dozen round tables where black men sat with glasses of beer. Overhead, four huge fans circled lazily, dispersing tobacco smoke into a uniform haze. There was a steady, even babble of sound and movement from the customers who filled the tables and played pool. As Hayes let his eyes grow accustomed to the light, he saw faces turning to examine him, then turn back to their cards and conversation.

Hayes knew that these taverns or speakeasies were illegal, yet openly tolerated throughout Soweto. They were called *shebeen*. The younger generation of Africans hated them, and it was easy to see why. Benches lining the walls held a variety of old men in shabby clothes, most of them passed out or asleep. The out-

of-work and the broken down gathered here to dull
their senses with the blessed mercies of beer. There was
consequently never a shortage of customers for the
shebeens. But revolutionary movements were often
tinged with self-righteous puritanism, something
Claude Hayes had always hated.

Aware of the whole room but not looking anywhere directly, Hayes slowly crossed the room to the
long bar. He squeezed in between two silent men who
seemed to alternate between staring into their beer and
staring into the dusty mirror behind the bar.

The bartender approached and addressed him in the
Xhosa dialect. Hayes could understand it, but not
enough to speak it himself. He answered in Swahili,
ordering a beer in the almost universal language of
Africa. The bartender put it wordlessly on the counter,
and Hayes sipped at the watery, bitter liquid. A strip
of flypaper hung down from the ceiling to eye level.
He regarded the bottom fly caught on the sticky roll.
It was a big fat one, hopelessly mired in glue. It buzzed
angrily and struggled against the death trap.

Hayes turned to face into the room and scanned the
faces in the crowd. He was definitely being watched
and studied now. Some of them wanted to rob him.
Some just wanted to know who he was. One of them
had something he wanted. It was just a matter of
finding the right person and gaining his trust. It was
easier said than done.

One tiny old man with bright eyes stared at Hayes
from a nearby table and made no attempt to conceal
his interest. His limbs were as thin as twigs and his
long bony fingers and wrists were laden with rings and
bracelets of metal, ivory and beads. Around his neck
he wore a chain of animal teeth. A tiny, feathered cap
was placed securely on the crown of his head. He

spoke a few words to the other men at his table, and they burst into uproarious laughter, with the old man glancing back twice at Hayes. His smile was a thin crease in the deeply lined black face. His cheeks bore the vestiges of tribal tattoos carved into his skin as a young man decades ago.

He pushed himself out of his chair, grabbing a great cloth bag with woven Ndebele designs on it. He rummaged briefly inside and pulled out a stick a foot long, hung with bangles, bracelets and other jewelry. He went straight for the stranger in town.

"You like my things. You must buy!" the old man wheedled in heavily accented Swahili. "For a great warrior, they will bring magic power."

Hayed smiled and looked at the old man. His eyes were blue, undoubtedly the result of a wayward white man's gene some generation back. He looked at the cheap jewelry the man held out, shaking his head slowly.

"No, I cannot buy your jewelry today."

"But you must," the old man persisted. "It's good jewelry. Here. For you." He pulled a wooden bracelet off the end of the stick and held it up. The band had been carved into the heads of two lions who looked as if they were kissing.

Hayes smiled and shook his head.

At that moment there was a yelp from the doorway. Just as he looked up, half a dozen young men leaped from their chairs and ran for the door in the back of the *shebeen* as a group of white South African policemen in short-sleeved tan uniforms burst inside.

The men who had tried to escape flew back into the *shebeen* with more police behind them. They were quickly thrown up against the wall. Conversations ended. Laughs and smiles died. Faces became grim, and bowed low over the tables. Shoulders sagged as if a great weight had descended upon them. A stony silence filled the Soweto tavern, cut by the ridiculous snore of an oblivious drunk, passed out on one of the benches near the wall.

The policeman with the most stripes on his shoulder walked slowly into the room, flicking his leather crop onto the palm of his hand. He snapped his fingers at the men standing at the pool tables, and they sullenly threw their cues down and returned to their seats.

"We're looking for someone," the police commander announced to the captive audience. "A man named Mthuli Sowanni. Anyone know where we can find him?"

His question was answered by silence.

The police commander waited, pacing arrogantly. "All right, then. We'll look for him. Get your passbooks out!"

The policemen behind him fanned out through the room.

The six men who had tried to run were being roughly frisked, one by one. The first had already been found without papers. He was handcuffed and led outside.

Hayes swallowed. He was watching a flash preview of what was going to happen to him within about thirty seconds. It was a major criminal offense for a black man not to have papers in South Africa. Without papers, police assumed they'd found a terrorist or troublemaker. In the circumstances, it was a generally valid assumption.

Already a young policeman was efficiently going down the line of men at the bar. He scrutinized each man's face with a steely glare, glanced down at the photograph in the passbook and reexamined the man's face again. Wordlessly he passed the ID back and moved on to the next.

Three people down the bar from Hayes, a young Bantu in a shabby black suit tore across the room for the open door. He didn't make it.

Two policemen threw themselves at him in a running tackle. The man kicked them, his hands flailing at the floor as he tried to drag himself outside. A fist rose into the air and smacked down loudly into his face.

Hayes stiffened, adrenaline exploding through his body. If he was going to get it, anyway, he figured he might as well go down fighting. The two policemen had the young Bantu up off the floor. One held his arms behind his back while the other laid into his stomach, both fists flying hard. The young man's eyes rolled up as his face contorted with pain, and saliva streamed from his mouth.

The head policeman grabbed a handful of the man's hair. "I think we have found Mthuli Sowanni," he said, in a teasing singsong voice. "Search the rest of them," he ordered his men.

Hayes was ready. He moved to throw himself into the fray when a steel hand clamped around his wrist.

"Wait!" The thin little man's grip tightened, and Hayes felt something pushed into his fingers. Paper. The hand let go of his wrist. The little man stood beside him, humming a strange staccato tune and staring off into space. He clutched his stick of bangles and bracelets in one hand and his identification papers in the other.

Hayes looked at the papers he had been handed. It was a passbook.

"I'll take that."

The white policeman snatched the little book from Hayes's hand. He nailed Hayes with a hard stare, flipped open the pages and examined the photograph. He flicked his eyes up at Hayes once again, shut the little book and handed it back.

"It appears to be in order," he said. He turned and started on the next man.

Hayes held the passbook in his fist. He was stunned. While the policemen were hustling handcuffed Africans out the door, the little man beside him kept humming nonchalantly.

Hayes flipped open the passbook in his hand. It was made out for someone named Gatsha Qoboza. But the photograph was familiar. It was Hayes.

"All right! You Bantus on that side of the room can move out now!" The police lieutenant shouted his commands with drill-hall authority.

"They separate the wheat from the chaff."

It was the little man beside Hayes who had spoken. Hayes looked at him and the man smiled, revealing a chaotic arrangement of his remaining teeth. "And the wheat is taken off to jail."

"Let's go!" the head policeman yelled again. "If your papers have been checked we want you out of here."

"Will you follow?" the little man asked deferentially.

Hayes nodded.

"My name is Samora."

Outside on the sun-scorched Soweto street, a crowd had gathered. Women carrying children and baskets of produce from afternoon shopping anxiously searched the faces of the men leaving the *shebeen*, seeking husbands, sons and lovers. Shouts and jeers of derision went up from the crowd as the police hustled another black man into a paddy wagon. Across the sea of black heads, fists were raised in the black-power salute. A woman screamed in anguish as her man was led away in handcuffs. She called to him and pushed her way to the front of the crowd, but a policeman shoved her roughly back as the man disappeared into the van.

"What will happen to them?" Hayes asked the little man as they pushed through the crowd outside the *shebeen*.

Samora shrugged. "Some who left their papers at home will eventually be released. Some who are on the lists for suspicious activities will be interrogated. Some will be detained, some will be jailed. A few might go to trial. One will die."

"Die?"

"They tell us our people commit suicide in prison but when we see the bodies we find many bruises. It is a difficult time for our people."

Samora pushed through the jostling angry crowd and turned down a narrower street that led away from the main road. The buildings here were residential, small brick bungalows with tiny front yards. The street turned and stopped where several more led off it. Samora chose one, turned at the next corner and turned again. Hayes was soon completely lost in the Soweto labyrinth.

Finally Samora stopped before a little brick house with a wooden porch. Over the doorway hung two enormous horns of an impala.

Suddenly it dawned on Hayes. Samora was a healer, shaman, astrologer, psychic. A witch doctor. The horns above the door were the trademark of his profession.

"Yes," Samora confirmed as if reading Hayes's thoughts. In fact, he watched the American's eyes. Hayes knew some of the tricks the healers and magicians of Africa used to make themselves appear powerful. But he'd also seen them do things for which no European or American had any explanation. In the *chimurengas* of Zimbabwe and Mozambique, freedom fighters often consulted with the witch doctors and village mediums for strategic advice. And they were highly supportive of the cause of African freedom from colonial powers. For one thing, it reduced the threat of competition with Western medicine.

Samora held the door open and motioned for Hayes to enter. As he crossed the doorstep he knew he was walking over a *muti*, a special wand hidden under a board that assured success and protection—and killed those who violated the witch doctor's sanctuary.

The darkened, cool interior was clean and simple. On the wooden floor of the large room, the hides of a zebra and a leopard were spread as rugs. On one side, a little table held candles floating in bowls of oil and braziers with smoking coals. Shelves held rows of jars and small clay pots filled with powders, leaves and dried withered things. The air was pungent with the cloying sweet odor of some burning herb or incense.

Samora went immediately to the little altar and threw some powder into a brazier. He muttered a low incantation and a sudden puff of smoke billowed up from the coals and dissipated. The sweet smell grew momentarily sharper.

"And with what magic did you create this?" Claude Hayes held out the passbook.

Samora turned from the altar, smiling secretively, his strange blue eyes dancing.

"There is a legend among the peoples on the northern border of Azania," Samora began, using the Bantu name for South Africa. He looked at Hayes. "The legend of a warrior named Kwati Umba, who dies in battle that he may return to life to fight again. No one knows where he comes from, when he will appear, or where he will go next. But it is said that sometimes he takes the shape of a panther to travel great distances. That he can live in the jungle, kill his enemies silently, swiftly, tearing their bodies into a thousand pieces. But that is just a legend. Kwati Umba is many people with many names."

Samora put his hand on the cover of Hayes's new passbook. "This belongs to a man whose name is Gatsha Qoboza, who lives in the Southeast Townships."

"And the photograph?"h

"I do not know everything, Gatsha. I received the photograph and was told that the man in the picture required certain papers. I am to help you in any way I can."

Hayes did not press Samora with further questions. On the long journey from the northern border to Soweto, he had been observed, studied, perhaps even recognized, all unknown to him. And somewhere along the way, he had been photographed. The picture in the passbook was recent, probably taken after his arrival in Vanda. He was looking straight into the lens of a camera he had never even seen. The background had been airbrushed white. The printing job on the forged passbook looked letter perfect.

"Not my best job," Samora commented with amusement. "But I had so little time to prepare it. You must tell me what else you need."

"A work permit. So I can work in the Krudd diamond mines. And a tattoo. I will show you what to draw."

Samora held up his hand to stop Hayes from speaking further. He strode to the door and bolted it securely. Then he pulled blinds down over the windows. The room fell into darkness, lit only by the sun's glow around the edge of the blinds and the candles on the nearby table.

Wordlessly, Samora yanked the leopard skin away from its place on the floor, revealing a trap door. He descended on a ladder that led into darkness.

"Come," he commanded.

Hayes climbed down into the hidden cellar just as Samora lit a kerosene lamp and replaced the glass chimney. The light flickered briefly before steadying, casting a rotation of shadows along shelves filled with potions, herbs and books. Hayes eyed some of the titles. They were books on Western medicine and philosophy.

"I used to study at the university—European medicine and philosophy. I found little there that we, the Bantu, did not already know in some form or another."

"So you chose to be a witch doctor in Soweto?"

"My mother was a medium and my father was a witch doctor. But I did not choose. The government did. I have been forbidden to attend university. In fact, I have been forbidden to leave Soweto."

Samora seated himself at a long table covered with papers, drawing instruments and inks of different colors. He carefully placed some tiny wire-rimmed glasses over his nose and pulled the coiled arms behind his ears.

"Your passbook, please."

Hayes handed it to him and looked over the little man's shoulder as Samora placed the identification papers on the long desk. In front of him was another printed card, a blank permit for a black worker to enter Johannesburg and seek employment.

"We will begin with this because it will take time. Then we will see to the tattoo," Samora said. He picked up the pen and set to work.

7

The 747 from London began its descent over Zimbabwe, the big puffy clouds scudding along at twenty thousand feet, casting their shadows across the African jungles below. The Limpopo River was a silver snake, wriggling through the dark greenery of the trees.

Nile Barrabas settled back in his seat as an excited hubbub rose from the other passengers.

"There's the Limpopo," a voice ahead exclaimed in delight, and a mother at the back of the plane explained to her restless child, "We'll see the mine dumps soon and then we'll be home in Johannesburg."

Beside him, Alex Nanos, "the Greek" as they sometimes called him, was still trying to get the flight attendant's phone number. The thrill of the hunt spurred him on. He knew goddamn well that once Barrabas had him and the rest of the mercenaries off the plane, they'd be too busy for extracurricular activity.

In the seat in front of them, Lee Hatton sat with Geoff Bishop, the ace Canadian pilot who could fly anything from an F-16 fighter to a chair mounted on a propeller.

The mercs had rendezvoused in New York a day earlier, where Bishop had joined them from Canada, and Nanos arrived at JFK tanned and smiling from one of his purposeful debaucheries in the Caribbean.

Twenty-four hours later they were descending to Jan Smuts Airport outside Johannesburg.

As for Erika, she hadn't just checked out of the hotel. She had checked out of Barrabas's life. The note left behind made clear what Barrabas had realized when he walked into the midtown lounge to see Jessup and Hatton. He phoned Amsterdam. She wasn't home. He left a message with her good-natured brother Gunter. He sent a telegram that would be waiting for her when she got there. In his mind's eye he kissed her goodbye forever and told his heart he didn't want to hear about her ever again.

When he closed his eyes he saw red. In this condition people who got in his way got hurt. It wasn't a great way to start a mission. Thinking with his fists had gotten him into bad situations before.

He sighed and folded his arms across his chest as the earth came closer.

"Your drink, Mr. Nanos." The flight attendant brought Alex another ginger ale. Alcohol was out of the question, considering the upcoming job, but he had to have some excuse to keep the lovely brunette coming back to his seat.

"Alex. Please call me Alex," the Greek begged.

"Alex." She smiled like a time-lapse rose coming into full bloom and set his drink down. Then she started down the aisle.

"Don't go yet!" Nanos thought quickly for another excuse to delay her. "Uh, have you got anything to, uh, nibble on?"

He winked.

She winked back.

"How about some nuts?" She set a little bag of candied peanuts beside the ginger ale.

Barrabas smiled at the sparring.

"Uh, that wasn't what I had in mind," Alex said, looking up with big innocent eyes. "How about the name of your hotel in Joburg."

"I'm sorry, Mr. Nanos. We're not allowed to give out that kind of information." She threw him a last teasing smile and moved away.

Nanos sat a moment, obviously disappointed. He turned to find Barrabas staring at him.

"Struck out." The Greek shrugged matter-of-factly.

"Happens to us all," said Barrabas. "Take a look." Barrabas pointed to the view out the window.

The airplane was down to ten thousand feet. Below them, the high veldt stretched away to the horizon. A crescent moon of hills and rocks a hundred miles long swung across the earth from east to west, and in the center of it, still far enough away to be barely a splotch on the landscape, were the towers of Johannesburg.

"The Witwatersrand," Barrabas told Nanos. "The richest gold fields in the world."

"I don't see it," Nanos said, craning past Barrabas to look.

Already the mine dumps around the city were visible. The tailings from the gold mines formed man-made mountains of yellow and white sand around the city, creating a physical barrier between the ranks of steel-and-glass office towers and the vast array of tiny houses stretching across the veldt southwest of the city.

Lee Hatton stuck her head up over the back of her seat. "Did you see that? Soweto."

Barrabas nodded.

"Who are these friends of yours exactly?" Nanos demanded.

"Not friends, exactly. Acquaintances of the family. Wilhelm Krudd knew my father in his capacity as a general in the U.S. Army."

The mercs had secret official status as observers of the South African security arrangements for Bishop Toto. Accordingly, their arrival was anticipated by the authorities. The faceless bureaucrats in Washington who had made the arrangement did not fail to notice an old alliance between Lee Hatton's late celebrated father and the wealthy and powerful Wilhelm Krudd. The mercs were scheduled to meet with Bishop Toto and the director of state security at the Krudd estate that afternoon.

Lee Hatton turned and sat down again, letting her weight fall against Geoff Bishop, who sat in the aisle seat in front of Nanos. Bishop was a tall, broad-shouldered man with a dark complexion and dark curly hair. He was the newest member of the team, and probably the least crazy. Years of flying commercial jetliners had given him nerves of steel.

Lee's hand slid down his arm and grasped his fingers.

"What are you going to fly this time, Geoff?" She made a flirtatious joke out of the question. He gave her a wry smile and noiselessly mouthed the word "You." Lee almost burst out laughing.

The big secret that everyone knew about but no one spoke of was that somewhere along the way Lee Hatton and Geoff Bishop had decided to become lovers. But when they were on the job, it was strictly business. The only one ticked off by the relationship was Alex Nanos, a fiercely loyal and protective man who was easily given to irrational jealousy.

Bishop cleared his throat and tried to look serious. "A helicopter, this time around. I'm hoping for a nice little secondhand Huey on loan from the security police.''

She leaned over and kissed him lightly on the mouth. ''Last one,'' she told him. ''The job begins when the wheels hit the runway.''

Moments later, they did.

The American mercs stood up and joined the rest of the passengers, grabbing their luggage from overhead racks and shuffling up the long crowded aisle. At the exit, the flight attendants formed a farewell line, smiling and nodding mechanically at the departing passengers.

One by one the mercs went through the ritual, shaking hands as the attendants said goodbye. Alex spied the luscious brunette in the lineup. Ignoring the others, he thrust his hand forward.

''Goodbye. It was wonderful,'' he said sincerely.

She narrowed one eye slightly and shook his hand. ''Thanks. Goodbye.'' Then she coolly turned to the next passenger, leaving a little slip of paper in the palm of Alex's hand.

As Nanos looked at it, Lee Hatton reached back and grabbed his shoulder.

''Come on, Alex.'' She pulled him out the door of the plane and onto the covered ramp that led into the terminal. ''What do you want to do, give her away?''

Nanos stopped and looked at the little card. On it was printed the name of a hotel, and below that was the elegantly written name of the flight attendant. Dianne Dionne. ''Whoooo—'' Nanos started to cheer. He was still blocking other departing passengers, and Lee elbowed him again.

''Alex! She'll lose her job if everyone hears you!''

The Greek was never known for his subtlety.

He plunged the paper into his trouser pocket and noticed Barrabas looking his way.

Ahead of them, control officers were ploughing through suitcases, valises, purses, handbags, knapsacks, wallets and anything else that attracted their attention. They were particularly interested in some books that they pulled from the luggage of various travelers. A woman was arguing vociferously about a thick volume that the officers wanted to confiscate.

"It's like going to Russia," said Hatton.

"Worse," Barrabas pointed out. "There are two kinds of lineups here." The rest of them looked. Half the room was taken up by white arrivals. On the far side of the customs area, one control desk had a long line of blacks only.

"Colonel Barrabas?"

Barrabas turned in the direction of the voice. A stiff young man in a security uniform stood at attention.

Barrabas looked him up and down. "Yes?"

"I'm from the airport security office, sir. I'm to escort you through customs. If you'll follow me."

The man led off without waiting for an answer, and a moment later the mercs found themselves in a private lounge.

"You will wait here," the young soldier informed them. "My commanding officer will be present in a moment."

The magic words had been spoken.

Another door opened and an older man with gray hair, wearing the crisp uniform of the South African security police, entered. Four customs officers followed. Behind them, a black porter wheeled in a dolly with their luggage.

"Colonel Barrabas, I'm Major Dik. Welcome to South Africa. I have been fully briefed of your status in this country. If you and your colleagues will just present your passports, these men will examine your luggage. Then you may go. There is a car waiting, as instructed, for you to drive to your hotel in Johannesburg.''

Dik motioned the customs officers forward, and they attacked the luggage like vultures on a ripe corpse. A few minutes later the mercs hardware was laid out on a table. Four broken-down Uzis, a Colt 45 and two Browning Hi-Powers lay side by side with enough 9mm ammo to stop a couple of paddy wagons and the follow-up car.

The security officers watched as the collection grew. No one talked. The mercs looked at one another uncomfortably, barely suppressing their annoyance.

The customs officers finished by pulling a couple of paperbacks from Lee Hatton's bag and throwing them on the table with the guns.

Lee shrugged. ''I was just reading up on your country, since I was coming here.''

''Yes,'' Major Dik said. ''Unfortunately the author of these books is banned in this country, which means his work is not available as reading matter. Now about the guns—''

Barrabas interrupted quickly. ''I suggest you put them back where they were found. Otherwise we go back to New York.''

His voice was stern, uncompromising.

''I will consult with my superiors,'' Major Dik said icily.

''Do that.'' Barrabas glared.

The major went to the telephone on the wall near the door, and a moment later was conversing rapidly in Afrikaans with someone. It was a language of South African whites that had evolved from that of the original Dutch settlers. None of the mercs spoke it or understood it. The major was silent for a moment, waiting for the word from higher up. His eyes darted back and forth between the Americans and their guns.

"Ja," he answered. *"Ja, goot. Dag."* He hung up and turned to Barrabas. His expression was icy with defeat.

"You may keep your guns." He snapped his fingers at the customs officers, and they put the weapons and ammo back in the American's bags. But not the books. The South African security officer wasn't finished, either.

"A warning, Colonel Barrabas. Our government welcomes representatives of foreign governments who come as observers. But agents provocateurs are not looked on kindly. They are not tolerated; indeed, they are eliminated. Do not oppose the regime."

Major Dik turned stiffly and left the room.

The young officer handed Barrabas a set of car keys, holding his chin high as if there was a bad smell in the room.

"Funny," said Barrabas. "I smell it, too. But I think the source of it just left."

The corporal looked at Barrabas oddly. He didn't understand the joke. "If you will follow me, I will show you to your car."

They grabbed their bags and went after the corporal through the crowded terminal. Outside, waiting in a VIP parking lot was a dark blue Ford. The corporal motioned to it, and without a further word walked back into the terminal.

Barrabas looked at the golden towers of Johannesburg rising above the mountains of mine tailings. "Welcome to South Africa."

"Some welcome," Nanos commented. "There's not even a driver."

"Yeah," said Geoff Bishop. "I hope there's a road map."

AN HOUR LATER, the mercenaries had checked in to the two-story penthouse suite of a modern hotel in the commercial district of downtown Johannesburg. The view from the plate-glass windows looked to the southwest, where the black townships sprawled across the veldt. Far in the distance lay the Drakensberg, the mountain range that shielded the interior of the country from the tropical coast on the Indian Ocean.

Their uncordial welcome continued to entertain them. On the way into the city, Barrabas felt around under the dashboard and seat until he found a hidden microphone. A similar, though more cursory, search of the hotel suite yielded three more. There were undoubtedly others. The Bureau of State Security was prepared for a show, and the SOBs were the star performers.

Barrabas stood outside the entrance to the hotel in a tan safari suit. The epaulets on the shoulders and the outside pockets on the pant legs lent a military look, but because this was Africa he stood out no more than any other tourist going for a one-day excursion to a wildlife preserve. He held a dark jacket over his shoulder to conceal the holster housing his favorite Browning.

He puffed on a small cigar and waited for the others to gather for their departure and afternoon appointment at the Krudd mansion.

The street in front of the hotel ran through the heart of Johannesburg's financial district. It was filled with shoppers and businessmen. The only black Africans were some maintenance men cleaning out litter bins in a park across the street. A sign over the gate indicated the park was for whites only.

"Like waking up in a nightmare, isn't it, Colonel?" Geoff Bishop said as he joined Barrabas.

Barrabas nodded, his teeth clamped on the cigar. "Yeah. It's hard to believe they call themselves a civilized country here. Ever been north of the border?"

"Zimbabwe?"

"Anywhere in Black Africa. I have. I used to fight in the mercenary wars there. The Africans know this country belongs to them, and the twenty million Bantus know that someday they'll take power away from the seven million whites who run the show. Right now they're waiting and watching and consolidating their power, but they say that if they have to, they'll drive the whites into the sea from the beaches of Cape Town. They mean it, too. Unless the whites change things first."

"Not much hope of that, is there?"

"None at all, I'd say."

Hatton and Nanos soon joined Bishop and Barrabas, and a few moments later the big Ford was heading northeast on the M-1, following the directions they had been given at the hotel. Traffic was light under a lemon yellow sun, and Barrabas settled back and let the hot dry African winds wash over him. Nanos was at the wheel. In the back, Hatton and Bishop watched the modern buildings of Johannesburg go by like an army of glass towers on alert and ready to march. Farther away, they glimpsed the summits of the ever-present mine dumps.

They had just passed the sprawling campus of the university when Alex noticed a large black American car on their tail and coming up fast.

"Colonel, someone's in a real hurry back there."

Barrabas reached out the window and adjusted the side-view mirror so he could watch.

The black car was traveling twice as fast as they were, pulling out from behind to pass.

"Don't let them get beside..." But even as he spoke, the car pulled alongside and slowed perceptibly to draw even with the Ford. The windows were shaded, but one in the back rolled down and a hand extended preceded by the dull metal snout of a gun. White fingers squeezed the trigger.

8

At the nearby Krudd estate, another car slowed to a stop in front of the mansion. Wilhelm Krudd left the big house on cue as Bishop Toto got out of the car. He appeared mildly put out.

"Bishop Toto! Welcome once again to my house!" Krudd said effusively.

"Mr. Krudd, I really don't understand why it was necessary for me to come here alone. It puts me in a very difficult position. That must be apparent to you."

"Of course." Krudd appeared apologetic. "But come inside and I'll explain everything."

The black bishop and the diamond industrialist went up the steps and through the big front doors.

"Yes, you had better explain what you mean," Toto told him, "about this assassination plot. And these security people from the United States."

"They are expected very soon," said Krudd. "Please come to the study." He led the famous cleric through the house to the oak-paneled room. Two security men waited there, their faces expressionless behind dark sunglasses. Wilhelm Krudd closed the door.

"Now what is all this about?" Bishop Toto demanded, his forehead wrinkled in annoyance. "I'm treading a very delicate line. My other visit here caused a great deal of controversy. I stand by what I said then, that my ministry embraces all people, black or white.

But please, Mr. Krudd, have no illusions about whose side I'm on.''

"I know," the conspirator said evenly. He snapped his fingers over his shoulder at the security men behind him, and they pounced with cool deliberation, grabbing the famous bishop's arms, spinning him around and snapping handcuffs on his wrists.

"This is an outrage!" Bishop Toto protested. His struggles didn't get very far. The security men pushed him against the wall.

"We've decided that you are too dangerous, Bishop Toto. We cannot allow you to...continue," Krudd said.

"You won't get away with this," Toto said angrily.

"We'll see," Krudd said as he walked to the door and opened it. "Major Snider!"

Sidney Snider walked slowly into the study, wearing a happy little grin.

The bishop and the director of state security recognized each other. It wasn't a happy reunion.

"I should have known you were behind this, Major Snider. You are one of my people's greatest enemies. You'll never get away with..."

Snider abruptly waved his arm outside the door. A short black man wearing a clerical collar and a dark suit, similar to the one Bishop Toto wore, entered the room.

The bishop's words froze in his throat. He was seeing a reflection of himself that might have stepped from a mirror to confront him.

"Surprised, Bishop Toto?" Snider taunted.

The religious leader gazed steadily at the impostor, who could not meet his fellow African's eyes. The actor looked instead from Snider to Krudd and back to Snider, shifting uncomfortably.

"No one will ever know that in two days time, our man here will wear the miter of the bishop of Johannesburg, not you." Snider's eyes glowed with evil intent. "Take him away," he instructed his men, "to his new home in the ground."

"I shall pray for you. For all of you," Toto said, as if issuing a threat.

Snider burst into laughter. "Please do," he said finally. "After all, it's our god against yours."

"HOLD ON!" NANOS YELLED. He stood hard on the brakes, throwing the mercs forward. Barrabas stopped his forward momentum into the dashboard with his forearm. The brakes bit hard, and the tires screamed across the road. Nanos gripped the steering wheel, locking his elbows to keep the car under control as the front-wheel stress tried to pull the vehicle off the road.

The black car overshot them, and the man in the back seat was turning to lean his weapon out the window and shoot straight.

"Guns!" Barrabas shouted over the slamming wind and the screeching tires. Bishop was already scrambling in his shoulder bag and with the jacket Barrabas had thrown carelessly into the back seat. He threw his leader the Browning and grabbed his own.

Nanos got off the brakes and turned the car sharply left across the middle line of the road. The car protested with squealing tires. Barrabas stood on the seat and braced himself with one foot against the dashboard as the upper half of his body went out the window. He held the gun around the door, steadying with his left hand.

The man in the other car fired first.

The headlights on the left side of the Ford exploded in a spray of glass and chrome, and the debris

smashed back against the windshield. Barrabas closed
his eyes and ducked back inside the car as shards of
glass and metal clipped his face. The man fired again,
and the headlights of the other side blew.

Barrabas cursed and threw himself out the window
again, this time firing as he went.

The back window of the other car went white and
crumpled into glass diamonds as his bullet struck
home. The powerful car pulled forward and quickly
put distance between itself and the American mercs.
Nanos steadied the Ford and put his foot down on the
gas.

"Leave it," Barrabas ordered.

"Let him go?" The Greek couldn't believe what he
was hearing.

"Yeah. Let's pull over." He wiped his hand along
the side of his forehead where a bit of debris from the
blown-out headlight had stung his skin. His hand
came away bloody.

"Let's have a look, Colonel." Lee was leaning over
the front seat as Nanos slowly angled the car onto the
paved shoulder. Other traffic continued whizzing by
as if nothing had happened on the freeway.

"Okay, Dr. Hatton. But it's just a flesh wound," he
said with a wink.

Lee Hatton dabbed at the cut with a tissue. "You're
right. This time you were just nicked. I think your
shirt is worse off than you are."

Barrabas looked down. The right sleeve had been
shredded along the back by something sharp.

"At least it's only your shirt," Lee said. "A little
closer and it might have been the artery. Hold the tissue there until your head stops bleeding."

He dabbed the cut on his forehead a couple of times
and tossed the tissue out the window.

"Who the hell were they?" Bishop demanded.

Nanos brought the car to a halt, and the four mercs climbed out.

Barrabas leaned against the Ford and lit a cigar as Nanos gawked at the smashed headlights. He opened the hood for a quick look at the guts.

"What do you figure's going on?" Lee asked the white-haired colonel.

"Nothing too serious," he said, puffing slowly on the cigar.

"Serious! What do you mean not serious!" With a sorry smile, Nanos shook his head and rejoined the others. "Hope you don't mind my saying so, Colonel, but you're bad luck for nice cars."

Barrabas chuckled a little. The Greek was referring to what happened to a black T-bird of his in Florida a few months earlier. Barrabas showed up for a visit one day, and a few hours later the T-bird was full of bullet holes.

"What can I say, Alex. I'm a popular guy."

Alex nodded. "Right. On everyone's dance card."

"So what was that?" Bishop asked. "Our welcoming party?"

"They weren't out to kill us, that's for sure," said Hatton.

Barrabas nodded. "Just saying hello, I think. They want us to know what they're capable of if we get out of line."

"I'd like to show them what we're capable of," Lee muttered angrily.

"So would I," Barrabas seconded. "Is the car okay, Alex?"

"Yeah. No headlights, but nothing in the engine got hit."

"Then let's go visit Mr. Krudd."

The mansion was not difficult to spot once the SOBs found the exit off the freeway. The eaves of the great house could be seen rising above the foliage that covered the hillside, and the street-level entrance to the estate was well marked by the white security guards who patrolled with submachine guns and automatic rifles.

After checking their ID and talking to the main house, the guards let them through.

A short corpulent balding man stood on the steps of the house with two black servants behind him as they drove up.

"That's Wilhelm Krudd," Lee told them.

When they left the car, the black doorman got in to park it. Krudd came toward them with an effusive smile, his arms outstretched in a gesture of magnanimous hospitality.

"Welcome! You must be Colonel Barrabas. And Lee! How wonderful to see you again after all these years. I was so sorry to hear of your father's sudden death."

"That was five years ago," Lee pointed out.

"Yes. Terrible thing. He was a great man, Lee. A man all of us who believe in democracy and freedom must admire."

Krudd and the mercenaries shook hands all around. Barrabas pointed to the car as the doorman took it around the drive to the service area.

"We had a little accident on the way out here," he told the wealthy industrialist. "No headlights."

"How did that happen?" Krudd asked, his brow furrowing in great concern.

"A car pulled up alongside and someone shot at us," Barrabas said matter-of-factly.

Krudd shook his head in disgust and sorrow. "Terrible, Colonel Barrabas. It is a dreadful thing what these terrorists are doing to our country. They come from Zimbabwe and Mozam—"

"The hand that held the gun this time was white," Lee pointed out.

"White!" Krudd seemed surprised. "Well, of course the terrorists have sympathizers on all sides. Come inside. Sidney Snider, the director of state security, is here. He will conduct an exhaustive investigation, I assure you. And Bishop Toto is waiting to discuss the security arrangements with you. You'll be most impressed by him."

The mercs exchanged knowing glances when Wilhelm Krudd mentioned an official investigation. They followed him into the mansion, and a black servant silently closed the doors behind them. In the foyer, a huge Christmas tree seemed completely out of place in the summer weather.

"We maintain the old traditions," Krudd explained, seeing their surprise. He led them through the richly appointed rooms of the opulent mansion until French doors opened onto a stone terrace, which gave way to lawns and tennis courts. A small garden party was in progress. Half a dozen people sat in wicker chairs enjoying cocktails, while couples in full whites played tennis.

"The player on that court—" Krudd pointed to a man "—is South Africa's greatest. Perhaps the world's, if only..."

"If only the American world champion hadn't refused to play him in this country?" Barrabas finished for him. The tennis boycott of South Africa had been headline news only a few weeks earlier.

"Yes," sighed Krudd. "If only you Americans would understand the reality of our situation. We are making progress, you know."

"Really?" Barrabas said noncommittally. He surveyed the scene a moment before following Krudd down the steps from the terrace into the gardens. He ran through all he had seen since they had arrived a few short hours ago. Everywhere they went, black people worked silently as laborers and servants, opening doors, cleaning streets, making beds, taking cars away. Here on the lawn, black maids in starched uniforms arranged food in silver chafing dishes on a long table covered with white linen. Black boys in white jackets served trays of drinks. Another small coterie of boys not even in their teens stood watch by the tennis players and ran off quickly to recapture errant balls or take water to the players between serves.

The whites played their game, or sat leisurely in wicker chairs leading lives of what appeared to be indolent luxury. The only other kind of white man Barrabas had seen since their arrival had been the kind with guns—the men at the airport and at the gates of the estate. And the hand in the window of a car on the freeway.

There was only one black man who differed from the others. He was sitting with the rest of Krudd's guests, nursing a drink and wearing a clerical collar. The man's face was immediately familiar from the world press he had received. It was Bishop Toto.

The occupants of the lawn chairs rose to greet them as they crossed the lawn.

"Gentlemen, our American friends," Krudd announced. He went down the line of names, Bishop Bloemvaal, Sidney Snider, Pieter van den Boos, Henry Miller, Richard Krudd. "And of course—" Krudd

stretched out his arm toward the smiling man in the
clerical collar "—Bishop Toto, who is my houseguest
for reasons of his personal safety until the consecration on Saturday. These gentlemen, and the lady, are
the Americans who will observe the security arrangements for the ceremony. Please, sit!" he invited them.

A servant silently offered them glasses of white wine
from a silver tray, which each of them refused.

"Perhaps you'd prefer something nonalcoholic,"
Major Snider commented.

"Actually, yes," Barrabas said. "As long as we're
working…"

"But the consecration isn't until Saturday, Colonel
Barrabas," Bishop Bloemvaal said. "Enjoy our wonderful country until then. I'm sure you and Major
Snider will have plenty of time to go over the arrangements his agency has made."

Krudd cleared his throat, "Sidney, Colonel Barrabas and his people endured a most unfortunate encounter on the freeway out here."

"Really, Colonel? Would you care to explain?"

"A car pulled up beside us and someone shot out
our headlights." A hot-headed Alex Nanos broke in
angrily, not waiting for his leader's response. "And I
wanna know why."

"Indeed, why?" said Snider, fingering his wine-
glass. "You see the kind of problems we have in this
country that force us to take such extraordinary precautions for the safety of our citizens."

"Yes," said Barrabas. "I understand completely."
He had noticed the thin smile on Snider's face when
the freeway incident was mentioned.

"Of course," Richard Krudd began, "we really
have the situation under complete control." He looked
away from the mercs. His voice was cold and distant.

"But we welcome you as observers," said Snider. "If only to show your government that we are a fair people. I'll have my men look into the matter immediately."

Barrabas nailed Snider with a hard stare. The two men looked each other firmly in the eyes in an act of recognition. They were enemies and they both knew it. Snider looked away first, to watch the tennis games.

Barrabas looked at Bishop Toto. The slight black man was chatting with Lee Hatton.

"Bishop Toto," Barrabas said, "you've been even more controversial lately since your appearance here a week ago. And now you've decided to stay here."

"I was just chatting about that with your lovely colleague," the bishop said, smiling at Lee. "In time, all will understand. I love even those whom I disagree with. These people here are my friends, and although I continue to educate them—" he smiled at Wilhelm Krudd and the others "—we are in agreement on many things."

On the other side of the little gathering, Geoff Bishop leaned into a conversation Alex Nanos had started up with Bishop Bloemvaal.

"Hello, I'm the bishop," Bloemvaal said, introducing himself to the pilot.

"So am I," Geoff Bishop responded.

The plump little man looked puzzled but let it go by with the easy tolerance foreigners feign for Americans that allowed them to get away with practically anything.

"I was just talking to your friend about some of your fascinating adventures. Like the time the Libyan white-slave traders were vanquished and how the appreciative young women you freed were so very warm and hospitable after..."

Alex coughed, embarrassed at being caught in such a flagrant attempt at story telling. "Right, Bishop." He raised his tumbler of ice water high. "Well, here's one for the old Libyan white-slave-trade mission, right, Geoff?"

"Cheers." Bishop followed the Greek's toast.

A thin waspish man with pale white skin suddenly appeared, peering owlishly at them through thick glasses.

"Gentlemen," said the plump little bishop, "please meet my colleague, Dr. Henry Miller, director of the Institute for Separate Development Studies in Cape Town."

"Separate Development?" Geoff Bishop queried.

"Apartheid," Miller explained happily.

"Yeah, well, I don't know if I like all this 'whites here' and 'blacks there' kind of stuff." Alex Nanos was uncomfortable, looking around to avoid the two South Africans whom he obviously didn't like. "I had a good buddy who was a black guy. It means I can't even sit on the same park bench with him here."

"But isn't that just the problem?" Bishop Bloemvaal said. "The world doesn't understand what we're really trying to do here."

"Exactly," Miller chimed. "The system is humane and there's a great deal of flexibility built into it. Why just last month the home affairs minister noted the number of people who were allowed to change their racial status in order to marry. Five hundred and eighteen coloreds became white, fourteen whites became colored and nineteen Indians became Malay."

"Seventeen," the bishop interjected.

"What?" the director asked.

"Seventeen Indians became Malay. You said nineteen."

"Ah, yes. Quite right. As well, eighty-nine blacks became colored—colored means mixed race—and five colored became black."

Nanos looked at Geoff Bishop, shaking his head.

"Where are we?" the Greek asked.

Bishop thought hard for about two seconds. "A Monty Python show?" he ventured.

They looked at the bishop and the director, good citizens both. The director waxed on enthusiastically.

"Three blacks became Indians, one became an Asian and a Malay became Chinese," he concluded, satisfied. Then he thought again. "Or was it Vietnamese?" he asked the bishop.

"Chinese...."

"No, I believe it was Filipino."

The two SOBs walked away.

Meanwhile, over by the punch bowl Wilhelm Krudd was explaining to Nile Barrabas and Lee Hatton why Bishop Toto was his houseguest.

"It was felt by most concerned that Bishop Toto would be safer here while he waits his consecration. You must understand, Colonel Barrabas, that when the leader of a people chooses to follow a moderate policy, he comes under fire from both extremes."

"I wonder what extreme had us under fire on the way out here," Barrabas commented wryly, turning his gaze to the tennis games still in progress.

Krudd and Snider looked momentarily uncomfortable. A young man left the tennis court and wiped his sweaty face with a towel handed to him by one of the young boys.

"You must meet my youngest son," said Krudd to break the difficult silence. "Paul!" he shouted to the tennis player.

The handsome man walked across the grass toward them.

"Paul, come and meet some other Americans." Paul Krudd looked slightly inconvenienced but headed toward them. "Paul grew up in America with his mother, my ex-wife," Krudd explained. "He has only just returned to South Africa."

Paul was quickly introduced to the other Americans.

"I was just saying to them how much you enjoy your native country, even after a long absence in the United States," Wilhelm Krudd told his son.

"Yes, father. I certainly do." He turned to the other guests. "I hope you enjoy it as much as I do."

"Our guests have never been to a diamond mine, Paul, and I've promised them a tour. I'd like to take them personally tomorrow. Since you'll be at the mines, too, we can do it together."

"But father, I..." the son began in protest.

Wilhelm put his hands up to stop him. "Tut, tut, Paul. We must show them some of our famous South African hospitality."

"Okay," Paul said. "Tomorrow afternoon, then. Colonel Barrabas, the rest of you," he said curtly. "Enjoy your visit. You'll find South Africa full of surprises." His words were heavy with unconcealed resentment, and he turned and walked to the house.

"These American habits," Wilhelm Krudd mused. "I'm still not used to you people. Always so fast, so abrupt." He shook his head in disbelief.

But Barrabas had no difficulty understanding Paul Krudd's behavior. The entire encounter had been set against a wall of solid hostility.

Silence fell for a moment among the gathering, and Barrabas watched the South African tennis champion finish his game.

"He's an excellent player, isn't he?" Major Snider commented.

Barrabas nodded.

The champion player's partner, a young woman, made a wild serve and the ball soared over the next court and along the grass. The champion looked around for one of the young black boys to get it. There was only one, on the bench by the equipment hut, and his face was buried in a magazine. The champion whistled and ordered the boy to get the runaway ball.

He jumped to attention and quickly brought a new one to the court. The champion took it, then he slapped the boy across the face.

Barrabas stiffened and rose in his chair when he felt Lee Hatton's hand close down on his fist and tighten. He sat again, his body trembling with rage. Nanos and Geoff Bishop looked at him, waiting for a cue.

"Don't be shocked, Colonel," said Snider. "You've just seen a small example of why the Bantus are incapable of running this country. They're basically lazy."

Lee turned to Wilhelm Krudd, making no secret of her outrage. "Do you allow that kind of behavior here?"

Krudd looked nonplussed. "Ah, of course not," he said. He snapped his fingers and a white-coated black servant appeared at his elbow. "Matubu, take care of the young man over there," he ordered.

"Of course, sir." The servant silently disappeared.

A moment later two of Krudd's uniformed private police appeared in the gardens. They went straight to the young black boy and escorted him out of sight.

From the side of his eyes, Barrabas looked at Bishop Toto. Incredibly, the African religious leader appeared not to notice the scenario that had just unfolded before his eyes.

"Colonel Barrabas, don't you think—" Krudd began.

"No," Barrabas interrupted. "I don't think." He pushed himself out of his chair and stalked toward the house. The other mercs got up and followed.

As they strode back through the house, Lee Hatton pulled up beside Barrabas.

"Colonel, there's something very odd about Bishop Toto."

"What do you mean?"

"He didn't react."

"I know. I saw it, too."

Geoff Bishop spoke up. "He's not what I expected. The newspapers write him up as if he's a great leader of the blacks in this country, and the main hope for straightening this mess out. But that guy has no charisma, no..."

"Energy," Nanos gave him the word he wanted. "Just shows you how people can get hyped up by the media."

When they reached their car at the front of the mansion, Wilhelm Krudd was scurrying out after them.

"You must understand, things are very different in this country," the industrialist said, desperately trying to placate the offended American observers. "I'm very anxious for you to see the diamond mine, and to have many further conversations about the African problem."

Barrabas was tempted to say the problem was white. Something stank about the whole situation. He slammed his hand down hard on the hood of the car.

"What are we supposed to do?" he demanded from Krudd. "Stand around and watch that kind of thing go on? There are some things that offend Americans a lot." Krudd shifted around a few times on his feet and appeared genuinely apologetic.

"Okay," Barrabas said. "I'll be ready tomorrow morning."

9

A thousand feet below the surface of the earth, in the depths of the Krudd Diamond Mine, a long column of black workers trudged slowly in single file through a huge whitewashed cavern. They wore overalls and mining helmets, but many were bare chested, their dark skin beaded and glistening from sweat. They were Xhosas, Basutos, Pondos and Zulu, strong and healthy young men brought from their villages to work for a time in the mines.

When the workers reached the cavern, the line shifted into smaller groups. Men from different tribes took their lunch buckets and sat to eat. Conversation was a babble of different languages and dialects.

Near a small group of Xhosa men, one man sat alone.

It was Claude Hayes. He squatted in a corner and pulled a cold patty of spiced meat from his lunch box. The rough stone wall was cold, and he arched his back and arms against it to stretch the fatigue from his muscles. The salt embedded in his sweaty shirt stung the still-tender tattoo on his shoulder. He began to nibble slowly on the patty.

The papers that Samora had forged for him worked perfectly. The diamond mines were always looking for strong men to dig in the pits. He had been hired on the spot for six months and taken immediately to the native compound, where the workers lived in long wooden barracks until their terms expired. Unlike the gold miners, workers in the diamond mines were virtually prisoners in a setting not unlike a concentration camp. It was a system deliberately designed to eliminate theft and smuggling of the valuable gemstones.

The next morning he began to work on the first shift of the day, descending to a depth of more than a thousand feet into the ancient volcanic pipes where the precious stones had been formed under incredible heat and pressure a million years ago.

The work was backbreaking for anyone who was new to it. Supervised by white foremen, hundreds of workers went into the farthest reaches of the tunnels that wound through the volcanic pipe.

The blue diamond-bearing rock was broken from the walls, and shoveled into the railed tubs that carried it to a central lift. Day by day, the tunnels grew minutely longer. Hayes was glad he had maintained his body in good condition. But muscles didn't make up for the unfamiliar labor, or the mind-numbing monotony of the work.

According to Samora, the man Hayes was looking for, the missing connection to the cell that smuggled out the diamonds, would somehow find him. But there were a thousand workers in the compound working on three different shifts. It might take weeks. If, indeed, the man had not given up and left or had not already been arrested by the state security police.

A tall young man walked over to Hayes from another group.

"Can I sit with you, Gatsha?" he asked, using Hayes's assumed name.

Hayes nodded and pulled his lunch basket out of the way to make room. Peter Uthulu had befriended him in the barracks. He was a Zulu, from the Kwazulu homeland, as his height and the long slender bones of his arms and legs indicated.

"Nkono is after you," Peter commented, quickly eyeing an enormous barrel-chested Xhosa miner across the cavern. Ever since Hayes's arrival, Nkono had cast silent, malevolent looks at Hayes. They had not spoken a word.

"Why?" Hayes asked. "What does he want from me?"

"He is the chief right now at the compound. You are almost as big as him, so you are a threat. He wants to fight you."

"I don't want to fight him."

"You might not have the choice, Gatsha."

At that moment, Nkono turned and caught the two men looking at him. He grimaced and turned away to speak to several men beside him.

"What is the biggest diamond ever discovered in this mine, Peter?" Hayes looked carefully at the young man's eyes as he asked the question. There was no indication of surprise.

Peter shrugged. "Not big," he said. "The big ones come from Kimberley, which is hundreds of miles away."

"That is where the Star of Africa comes from, isn't it?"

Peter nodded without bothering to look up from his lunch. "Yes. The diamond that is among the crown jewels of the queen of England."

"It is said that the Star was only a small part of a much larger diamond. That the other half was discovered by black workers and smuggled out, to the mountains in the north."

Peter shrugged again and munched contentedly on his lunch. "That is an old story, Gatsha. If it's true, well, I have never seen this famous diamond that was spirited away. It's just a story."

Suddenly someone kicked the ground in front of them. A cloud of dust and grit flew into their faces. Both men looked up. Nkono was towering over them, his hands defiantly on his hips.

Hayes brushed the grit off his bread with his fingers and ignored the big man.

Nkono didn't move. The banter of lively conversation in the underground cavern hushed. All eyes turned to watch the challenge.

Hayes took a bite of his bread, and again Nkono kicked the ground, sending another flurry of grit and dust at Hayes.

The disguised mercenary stopped eating. He could feel rage spreading through his guts and down his arms to his fists. He wanted to avoid trouble, but he wasn't being given the chance.

"You want something, Nkono?" he asked, slowly and without looking up.

Nkono answered by kicking yet another pile of dust in Hayes's face.

Hayes paused a moment, then took a deep breath. He shifted his legs slowly until they were in the right position. There was only one way to deal with a troublemaker. Take him out with the first move.

Hayes threw himself forward, using the top of his head as a battering ram. Nkono wasn't ready for it. His stomach was soft at the point of impact with Hayes's hard skull. The big Xhosa grunted as the air was knocked out of him. He fell back, his eyes bulging in anger born of pain and humiliation.

The other miners in the room jumped to their feet and began to urge the fighters on with shouts.

Nkono clutched his stomach and faced Hayes, his nostrils flaring. Both men breathed hard, waiting for the other to move. They circled each other, their arms outstretched and ready. It wasn't going to be an easy fight. Nkono was forty pounds heavier and three inches taller. And the crowd was on his side.

The Xhosa motioned to someone on the sidelines. A miner threw him a wooden club two and a half feet long with a round knob on one end. He caught it with his right hand and whipped it hard at waist level in Hayes's direction. Hayes jumped back as it swung inches from his stomach.

Nkono moved forward menacingly, holding the club high over his shoulder. He swung it hard toward Hayes's head. The American put his forearm up to block it and Nkono stopped the momentum of the club and threw a left with his fist. It drove into Hayes's diaphragm. Then he slammed his club into Hayes's knee.

The American staggered back, the blow to his diaphragm and knee bringing tears to his eyes. He blinked rapidly to clear them, and tried to catch his breath. Nkono's followers were laughing at him. The blow to his knee was so hard that his leg was numb with pain and he almost fell.

Nkono smiled, savoring the cheers of the crowd, and stepped back to watch Hayes suffer.

Claude remained bent over, catching his breath, watching Nkono's feet for the next onslaught, telling his pain to go away. It didn't.

Nkono moved forward. Hayes straightened as the brutal man towered over him, the club raised back for the final blow. Again the American lifted his left forearm in a block. This time it worked. The Xhosa's hand hit Hayes's wrist, and the American twisted himself under his attacker's outstretched arm. He reached with his right and circled the limb, locking his right hand onto his left wrist.

Nkono drove his weight forward but it was too late. With Hayes's hands locked together around Nkono's arm, the American stepped back. Nkono strained to keep his balance, and the two men were locked in a battle of strength and skill, their sweaty bodies pressing into each other. Slowly, inch by inch, Hayes prevailed, pushing the African off balance. Nkono reached with his left to grab Hayes's neck. Hayes shifted. Nkono's fingers caught the neck of his T-shirt and ripped it.

The counterattack failed, and it gave Hayes the edge he needed. He grunted, summoning his remaining strength, and strained at Nkono's arm. The Xhosa's strength failed. He howled and twisted backward onto the hard rocky ground, pulling Hayes down with him.

Claude was fast.

As Nkono went down, Hayes's hands shifted from the arm to the club. He snatched the weapon from the African's hand and rolled backward, beyond Nkono's grasp.

Nkono came up like a wounded animal, his face streaming with beads of sweat, his eyes savage with fury from his humiliation. The rhythmic chant and clapping of the other miners dwindled to a stop as the intensity of the fight spread its shock wave through the crowd.

Nkono charged. He balled his fists and drove a hard right to Hayes's face, oblivious to the weapon that his opponent now held. A big mistake.

Hayes gave a short snap to the inside of Nkono's elbow. Nkono yelped with hot stinging pain, and Hayes grabbed the outstretched arm by the wrist. Like a cat, he slid behind the big African, pulling the arm with him into a half nelson. He shoved the club into the crook of the man's elbow and grabbed Nkono's other arm. Now the nelson was full. And the club made a perfect pry. Hayes levered it upward.

"Nooooo!" The big African howled in panic. A broken arm meant more than pain. It meant unemployment.

Hayes stopped, but kept pressure on the club that pivoted the arm upward into an impossible position. The two men breathed hard in exhaustion. Streams of sweat ran down their faces and arms and dropped onto the ground. Both men waited for the other to make a move.

Hayes got tired of waiting.

He pulled the club from the man's arms and pushed him forward. Nkono lost his balance and went down, sprawling on his belly in the dirt.

A great cheer rose from the crowd of mine workers, and many rushed forward in spontaneous dances of celebration, hooting and clapping Hayes on the back. One small knot remained to one side, glowering at their work mates and helping Nkono to his feet.

Peter crowded in behind Hayes.

"You have just beaten the shift chief. But Nkono and his followers will not take his defeat easily," he warned. He glanced down at the T-shirt that had been ripped during the fight, exposing Hayes's shoulder and chest. The head of the panther was clearly etched into the raw flesh.

A long whistle sounded in the cavern—the white foremen had returned to collect their work gangs. They stood at the entrance to the cave, calling and gesturing to the Bantu workers.

The young Zulu looked at Hayes, then pulled the flap of tattered cloth up to cover the tattoo. He turned slowly away, slipping his left hand to his right shoulder.

He pulled the sleeve up briefly. Long enough to reveal the head of a panther burned into the flesh.

"Come on! Let's go!" Another foreman shouted his orders and backed them up with a long hard blow on his whistle. "We have a special tour of VIPs coming through today, so let's look like we're working!"

His exhortations failed to excite the Bantu workers. They moved slowly into their work parties and began the long trudge back into the farthest tunnels of the diamond pipes.

As Peter joined his work party he looked back at Claude Hayes. They studied each other but gave nothing away.

Hayes had found his man.

"You! Come on, let's move it!" A foreman yelled at him. Hayes turned to go. Across the cavern, Nkono glowered at him, his dark eyes filled with hatred.

NILE BARRABAS STARED DOWN from the helicopter window at the landscape of the high veldt that rolled away from the cities of Johannesburg and Pretoria to the Drakensberg Mountains in the east. It was a beautiful, sunny day that offered perfect visibility of the rolling savanna, the sprawling suburbs of Johannesburg and the streets of Pretoria outlined with the purple blossoms of acacia trees. The pilot pointed out to the north the colorful brick houses of the Ndebele natives. To the south, Barrabas could see the round thatched huts of a Zulu village, spread around the kraal where the cattle were kept.

Back in Johannesburg, Geoff Bishop had been sent out to get a promised helicopter from the security police for the mercs to use. Lee Hatton and Alex Nanos were meeting with some of Major Snider's people to go over preliminary security arrangements for the consecration ceremony the next day. Barrabas went by himself to meet Wilhelm Krudd at the diamond mines.

"There it is, straight ahead. The Krudd Diamond Works." The pilot pointed ahead of them.

The highway below ended abruptly several miles to the east in a stretch of scattered buildings and high dumps of crushed rock. The complex was surrounded by several rows of electrified wire fence. The guard posts and jeep patrols along the perimeter of the complex were also obvious from the air.

To one side, inside the complex but surrounded by another high fence were rows of low wooden barracks. It was the African workers' compound.

The helicopter began its descent, and only a few minutes later the skids set down on a clay landing strip outside the main gates. A jeep with a driver waited to carry Barrabas the half mile distance to the gates of the mine.

As justified as it had seemed at the time, the colonel's departure the day before from the Krudd estate wasn't the best politics to use in the situation. But the man was never known for his diplomacy.

Nevertheless, he wanted to give the appearance that the mercs were trying their best to be neutral. He had the impression that this tour had been set up to convince him how good the whites were to the African workers. For the time being, he was willing to give Krudd the benefit of the doubt.

Pacing in front of the jeep, Paul Krudd waited for him impatiently. He scowled as Barrabas approached.

"My father couldn't come, after all."

"You don't sound too disappointed."

"I'm not," the young American-born South African said easily. "I'm not a daddy's boy. And I prefer not to conduct guided tours, quite frankly." His intimation was clear. Barrabas wasn't wanted. But being a mercenary wasn't a popularity poll. It was all the more reason to go.

"I wouldn't miss it for the world," the colonel said.

"Then if you're ready, we'll go straight into the mine compound," Paul said curtly. He opened the door and climbed into the jeep, behind the wheel. Barrabas got in the other side.

The jeep started down the gravel road that led to the mine gates.

"You don't seem very anxious to make this tour," Barrabas said, keeping his eyes ahead and on the road.

Paul turned briefly from the wheel and studied the white-haired warrior from America.

"No comment," he said.

"You just do what your father tells you to do."

"That's right," the younger Krudd answered quickly, his lips set in an angry line. "And my father told me to give you a tour of the mine so you can see how well we treat our workers. And that's exactly what you're going to get. Call it propaganda, call it whatever you want. You can't do anything about it. And you aren't going to."

Barrabas looked at the young man. He thought he detected a note of sarcasm in the other's voice, but he couldn't be sure.

Paul continued, his words sharp and to the point. "As far as I'm concerned, it won't do a whit of good with people like you. You don't understand the situation here. And you never will."

"Why? Because I'm not South African?"

"That's right," Paul answered quickly. "You're not. You're American."

"I thought you were, too."

Paul started to answer but stopped. His face tightened as he searched for a response.

"I used to be," he said. He threw a defiant look Barrabas's way. "But I'm doing something about it," he concluded enigmatically. "Unlike other people I know."

He slowed and braked at the twelve-foot-high wire gates that led into the main compound. Armed guards pulled the great gates back to let the jeep through. The men rode the rest of the way to the main building of the dusty compound in complete silence.

10

Claude Hayes dumped the last shovel of crushed rock into the bin and stood back. Another worker set his weight against it and pushed. The bin moved slowly and heavily forward on its metal rails, rocking down the tunnel until it slammed into another bin full of rock.

The workers dragged an empty bin forward. One down, another one to go. Without speaking to one another, the miners turned back to the tunnel wall and started digging again. Half an hour was left on the shift.

The work was heavy and monotonous, and the way to survive was to shut the brain down and go on automatic for eight hours. Hayes looked forward to the return to the barracks where he could stumble into a dead sleep. And dream of carts filled with rock sliding down long glistening rails through underground tunnels. It was an ordeal.

The white foreman had disappeared ten minutes earlier and had not returned from his inspections of the other work gangs. Hayes set his shovel against the rock wall and walked back down the tunnel to where the water canteens had been left.

He took a guzzle, rinsed his mouth and spat it out. In the gritty earth at his feet a couple of pebbles lay like bits of soapy glass. He picked them up and bounced them in his hand. Raw diamonds, worth a thousand dollars apiece on the carefully controlled world market.

"Gatsha!"

Hayes jumped at the sound of his name. Suddenly Peter Uthulu was at his side.

"What are you doing here?" Hayes asked with alarm. Peter belonged to another work gang stationed in a different part of the mine. If he was caught he would be in trouble.

"The son of the man who owns this mine comes to inspect the pipe and the conditions down here," Peter explained quickly. "Today he has brought an important visitor from America." He said the last word almost in sorrow. "All the white foremen have gone to the cage to see. Quickly—we have little time. You must follow me."

Without waiting for an answer, Peter turned down the tunnel. Hayes hesitated only a moment, looking around to make sure he was unobserved.

Peter led him back to the main gallery. The great whitewashed cavern was empty. The heavy rumble of carts sliding down their rails echoed like heavy thunder through the underground passages. Peter darted over the rails that ran down the center of the gallery and hopped around trains of bins piled high with the crushed diamond-bearing rock.

Finally they came to a secondary passage that was closed off by a wooden barrier and a huge piece of mine machinery, its engine torn out to be repaired. Peter squeezed past the barrier and disappeared behind it.

The tunnel on the other side was dark. Peter snapped the light of his helmet on.

"This tunnel has been exhausted," he told Hayes, adding, "they think."

The Zulu set off again, the light from his helmet leading them into the darkness. The air became warm and stuffy as they neared the end of the tunnel.

Soon they stopped. Peter turned to Hayes.

"I have been waiting for you to come," he said. "In two weeks my term of employment is up. Will you replace me? Why has there been such a long silence from the organization?"

"The cell has been broken," Hayes explained quickly. "The others have been taken prisoner."

"Then I am in great danger." Peter said it as if it were a simple fact of life. "Eventually their interrogation methods bring results."

Hayes nodded. "They found the border-contact zone," he told Peter.

"Then they have broken Chikorema, because only he knew of it. And why have you come?"

"To find you. And to find the New Star."

The Zulu warrior studied Hayes's face. "What tribe are you truly from?"

"I'm American."

Peter nodded slowly as if he began to understand something. "There is another reason. I see it in your eyes. I saw it when you came here yesterday. You have a fire that burns within. Is it called vengeance?"

"Does it not burn in you, too?" Hayes asked. "To be a slave like this?"

"Sometimes," Peter answered. "But victory burns brighter than vengeance, and the warmth of its fire lasts longer. There are white people who help us in our fight for freedom. How can I demand vengeance against those who can also be my allies? But come. I have something to show you. We can talk later."

He lowered himself to his knees and with his gloved hand began digging at the base of the tunnel wall. The earth brushed away easily, revealing broken rocks. Peter pulled them aside until his light shone on a large whitish rock. He scratched it. The surface glinted like glass. It was a diamond, still half buried in rock. But even the part that was exposed was the size of a football.

"The New Star," Hayes whispered in awe. It was worth tens of millions of dollars.

"It is the biggest diamond ever discovered," Peter explained. "We have known about it for months, and keep it hidden."

"All the workers know?" Hayes asked incredulously.

Peter shrugged. "Many of them. They will not tell because they know the white man will take it out of the country. And it belongs to us."

"How will you get it out?"

Peter laughed. "The person I pass the diamonds to can take it out. But it's more difficult because of its size." He took Hayes's hand in his and pressed it to his jaw. The American could feel hard lumps under the skin below the Zulu's teeth.

Peter laughed again. "And all this time I have talked, you never suspected my mouth was full of diamonds, did you!"

Hayes shook his head in disbelief. "But obviously you can't smuggle the big one out that way."

Peter took it as a very funny joke and slapped his knee, trying hard to laugh without making noise.

"No!" he said, his laughter stifled. "No. My contact will arrange for it. You will see. But we must hurry."

The two men quickly pushed the rocks and grit back into the gap in the wall to hide the huge stone.

"Tell me who your contact is," Hayes asked as they finished.

Peter's white teeth flashed in the smile that spread across his dark face. "Watch me," he teased. "And tell me if you see who I give the diamonds to. I will give you one hint. I will do it before we reach the inspection station."

"But…" Hayes started to tell the young Zulu it was too important to play games. But Peter had already begun his return down the tunnel.

As the two men approached the wooden barrier at the end of the tunnel, a long high-pitched whistle sounded to mark the end of their shift, and by the time they reached the barrier, the gallery was filling with hundreds of miners as the work gangs returned to the cages that would take them to the surface.

Hayes and Peter easily slipped unnoticed into the stream of men that poured past them. As they entered the high cavern where the lift was, they saw a party of white men in fresh clean overalls and white helmets standing in the crowd.

"The visitors," Peter whispered to Hayes. They pushed forward into the dense crowd of African workers.

A red light flashed over the lift door, announcing the arrival of the cage. The doors opened. Foremen moved in front of the surging crowd of black miners, blowing their whistles and pushing the workers back. The visitors were ushered forward into the cage.

Hayes saw their faces as they went aboard. The first one turned and scanned the crowds as if looking for someone.

"The one in front—that is Paul Krudd," Peter whispered to Hayes. "His family owns this mine."

Hayes nodded dully, hearing the words but not registering them. He was too shocked to see anything but the face of the white visitor.

It was impossible. But under the helmet of the tall man who followed Paul Krudd into the elevator, he recognized a face he knew.

Nile Barrabas.

The colonel. In the enemy camp.

BARRABAS STOOD UNCOMFORTABLY with Paul Krudd as the big cavern filled with workers during the shift change. The cage took forever to descend.

Just as the red light blinked, he saw something through the sea of black faces that jolted him. It was the face of a ghost. The man he was looking at turned to talk to the miner beside him. It was hard to be sure, with the overalls and helmets, but he could have sworn it was the face of Claude Hayes.

Impossible. Claude Hayes was dead.

"It's here, Colonel Barrabas." Paul Krudd extended his arm to invite him to enter the cage. The crowd of workers pushed forward, obviously eager to call the day over and get back to the earth's surface, where the air smelled fresh and the sun shone brightly.

He looked again for the man in the crowd, but the face had vanished into the others. The workers flowed into the cage, surrounding them, and the big elevator lurched and began its thousand-foot climb to the earth's surface.

The tour had been, for the most part, a boring waste of time. Paul Krudd had maintained an incredible animosity toward the American, hurrying him through the main complex above ground where tons of rock was poured into giant crushers, sifted for diamonds, which were then sorted, counted, weighed and packed for shipment to the cutting houses of Cape Town and Amsterdam.

The underground trip to the mine had been the most interesting. But even there, Barrabas felt the omnipresent weight of thousands of tons of earth and rock overhead, the claustrophobic quality of the great rock-hewn caverns and the stale artificial air the miners breathed.

"What will you do now?" Paul asked him.

"Tonight I have to discuss the security arrangements with my people."

"I'm sure Major Snider's arrangements will be quite secure. He's most efficient in his work."

"Krudd, everything you say can be taken at least two ways," Barrabas said sharply, his brow furrowed in annoyance at the young man.

Paul turned away from Barrabas without saying another word.

The cage halted and the doors opened at the surface. They waited as the hundred or so workers filed off into a large outdoor waiting area. It was enclosed on two sides by buildings that housed change rooms and showers, and on the third by the electrified metal fence hung with barbed wire. Uniformed guards patrolled the yard. Guard dogs strained at their leashes and barked at the workers leaving the cage.

"The workers have to strip and go into the showers. Their clothing is inspected by whites to make sure that no diamonds have been concealed. From the showers, they go naked into the change rooms to put their own clothes on. So you see, there's no opportunity for them to steal," Paul explained.

"Except for swallowing them," Barrabas suggested. "Or sticking them up their..."

"There are further security precautions in the compound. Before they leave at the end of their term with us, each worker is X-rayed."

As they walked out of the cage, Paul pointed to a door on the other side of the yard. "Go through there. I'll join you in a minute. I have to talk to some of the foremen."

He walked into the crowd of Bantu workers, heading for the gaggle of white foremen that stood to one side. Just then Barrabas caught sight of the tall muscled man he had taken for Claude Hayes a few minutes earlier. His eyes were riveted to him. The face was hidden, but something about the way the man stood and walked was intensely familiar.

Suddenly the door of one of the buildings flew back and a dozen brown-uniformed security police burst through. One of them yelled orders to the others and they fanned into the crowd, shoving the workers aside. The guard dogs around the perimeter of the fence began barking furiously, scenting trouble and terror. Bantu workers ran for the sidelines.

"There!" one of the police cried. "That one!"

The crowd of terrified workers suddenly swept away from the man the guard had pointed at.

A tall young miner with the long slender features of the Zulu tribe stood alone and isolated in the yard. He saw the guards rushing toward him, his face alive with fear.

His eyes swept the compound. There was only one way he could go. Over the fence. The young Zulu started running.

Paul Krudd suddenly reappeared at Barrabas's side. He was white with fear.

"What's happening?" Barrabas demanded.

Krudd shook his head slowly. "I don't know." He was very nervous.

The guards took off after the running Zulu, but the long-legged man had a head start on them. The distance between pursued and pursuers widened.

They unleashed the dogs, and the German shepherds bounded across the dusty compound with fangs bared. The fleeing miner didn't look back until the first dog reached him.

The killer beast jumped for him. As if by instinct, the Zulu stopped dead and went down into a momentary crouch. The dog overshot his mark and sailed over his head. The man was up again, swerving to the side and back toward the fence.

With an immense jump on his long legs, the Zulu leaped for the fence and grasped the topmost coil of barbed wire.

The wires sizzled and snapped. The lower part of the man's body crashed into the fence, his clothing snagging on the barbs that held him there.

He fried.

His body jerked and shook in spasms as the electricity jolted through flesh and muscle, boiling the blood in its veins. Blood burst from his skin and streamed down his body. His hair and clothing began to smoke. The body was limp. The dogs barked and jumped at the feet of the electric crucifixion. Guards yelled orders. The workers stared at the ground, their shame and anger smoldering in dark eyes.

The dead man's hand opened, spilling raw diamonds the size of marbles onto the bloody, dusty ground.

Barrabas looked at Paul Krudd. "Is this what I was brought here to see?"

Krudd turned to him, speechless and close to shock. "I...I..." He was at a loss for words. "Let's get out of here." He pushed blindly through the door into the mine building.

Outside, the foremen yelled at the workers to go into the change room. Slowly they shuffled forward through the door and began to strip. In a control room somewhere, the current through the fence was turned off. Half a dozen workers were conscripted to disentangle the body from its grisly trap.

"Come, you! Get going! And stop your staring!" The policeman was yelling at the tall heavyset man who watched Peter Uthulu's body being carried from the compound.

Claude Hayes looked at the policeman with a hatred that frightened him. Then he walked through the door into the change room to strip off his mining gear. His hands were shaking as he removed the helmet and the gritty overalls.

It was definitely Nile Barrabas, walking with the son of the guy who owned the mines. What the hell was he doing here? It had to be a mission of some kind.

Christ, he thought. It's a helluva time for our paths to cross. But whose side is he on? That was the million-dollar question. When he was with the SOBs, they usually took the job for the money and made or demanded whatever concessions were required along the way.

So what was Barrabas up to now, he wondered.

As for his own mission, he had no doubts whatsoever.

Naked, he joined the other workers crowding into the huge shower room, and put his head under the hot spray of water.

With Peter's death, he was now the only contact who knew the location of the biggest diamond ever discovered. And just before the guards came after Peter, he had seen something else.

He saw Peter pass a first handful of diamonds.

The soothing water jetted down into his face, calming him.

Now he knew how diamonds were smuggled out of the Krudd mines.

11

The black man who sat in the chair in Major Snider's office sweated and shook with fear.

The irons on his legs and the manacles on his wrists had cut deeply into his flesh, making him bleed. His face was bruised. He sat with his shoulders hunched and his head down, not daring to look at the man who stood over him, the man asking questions.

"You've been good so far, Mthuli," Snider said kindly. He stood with his arms folded across his chest, looking down at the terrorist. "But if you don't tell me the rest of what I want to know, I'll have to give you back to Ernie and Johann."

The prisoner's trembling increased, but he said nothing.

The interrogation session was interrupted by the ringing of the telephone. Major Snider answered it and spoke quickly. "Very good," he concluded, and hung up.

He went back to the prisoner. "Your young Zulu friend, Peter, chose the easy way out. He was electrocuted on the wire fence when he made a run for it. So now it's up to you to tell us who he was supposed to slip the diamonds to."

Once again, the prisoner trembled. Still he was silent. Major Snider waited a few moments.

"Very well," he said wearily. He picked up the phone and pressed the intercom buzzer. "Have Ernie and Johann come into my office please. I'm going for dinner."

PAUL KRUDD CLIMBED BEHIND THE WHEEL of his red Ferrari and slipped it into gear. The little sports car roared out of the diamond mine's parking lot in a cloud of dust and a blur of speed. High above the road he could make out the tiny speck that was the helicopter carrying the American colonel back to Johannesburg.

He turned off the main highway onto Route 101 on the eastern side of Pretoria, avoiding the capital city and turning north until more signs pointed him off the highway in the direction of Athatsawana.

He reduced the speed of his Ferrari only slightly, despite the sudden potholes and crumbling asphalt of the road. Arid high veldt stretched away to the Drakensberg and Soutpansberg mountains in the east and north. Cactus, baobab and wild fig trees were the inhabitants of this countryside. The low shrubby trees grew thicker, the green of their leaves rich in the afternoon sunlight, as the rolling grassy plains gave way to the woodland bushveldt in the west and another small ridge of mountains called the Magaliesberg.

Finally he turned north on a road still worse than the one he just left, passing on his right an enormous pile of stones. He pulled the car over and stopped for a moment to gaze at the strange landmark that the Bantu called *isivivane*, or "lucky heaps." Found throughout Africa, they were the continent's most ancient highway signs, made over centuries by travelers on their way into Azania and Namibia. Each traveler added his stone to the heap and asked his gods for strength and good luck on the journey ahead.

Paul Krudd left his car and picked up a small rock from the side of the road. He heaved it with a hard underhand until it hit the top of the pile, bounced down a few feet and stopped.

The soft dry winds, perfumed by the flowering trees of the bushveldt, blew against his bare face and arms. The eastern horizon was just slightly darkened now, as the sun sank low in the west. There were clouds in the north. A rainstorm was coming up. He cast a final look at the *isivivane*. "Give me luck," he said to it. "We're going to need all we can get."

He returned to his car.

Ten minutes later he approached the frontier to the Athatsawana homeland.

The homelands were an essential part of the government's grand scheme of apartheid. They were little more than reservations for the confinement of African natives so the whites could exist by themselves in peace. The homelands were said to be independent—a mockery of truth belied by the absence of any international recognition of their right to self-government. South Africa's white government still controlled the police, the judiciary, the army and the economy—such as it was—in these barren places that comprised fifteen percent of the worst land South Africa had to offer. The homelands were arid, mountainous and completely unsuitable for farming. The city blacks were deprived of their citizenship, driven to the homelands and kept there in dire poverty on the edge of starvation with no possibility to leave and no legal right to enter the white-controlled areas of the country.

They weren't reservations. They were massive concentration camps.

The final solution.

Paul Krudd felt angry again. Since he had returned to South Africa he felt angry almost all the time. When he was a small child, his mother had divorced Wilhelm Krudd and returned to her native America. Disgusted by her own experience in South Africa, she had warned Paul what he would find there. The reality of it overwhelmed her words.

He braked in front of the armed guards at the frontier of Athatsawana. A handwritten sign tacked to the guard booth announced that one and all must show their passports.

A black guard in a South African army uniform, with the colors of the Athatsawana homeland sewn to his sleeve, came to the car window.

"Your permit, sir, if you please."

It was forbidden for whites to enter the homelands without permission from the South African commissioner of homelands. Such a formality was not a problem for a man with the family connections of Paul Krudd. His reason was simple. He collected Ndebele wood carvings.

"Ah, Mr. Krudd," the guard said, examining the papers and recognizing the status of the visitor. "Enjoy your visit, sir."

The guard stamped his passport, and Paul handed over the two-rand payment.

"Your documents, sir."

Paul looked at them quickly. One welcomed him to the independent state of Athatsawana. The other declared him a prohibited person under section 4(1) of Act 59 and threatened imprisonment if he dared to enter. The absurdity of it was so incredible he had to laugh.

The guard removed the iron barrier, and Paul drove out of South Africa into the homeland.

A few miles farther down the road he came to Sampane, the capital of the fake republic. Like Soweto, it was a sprawl of mud-and-brick houses roofed with corrugated iron. In the late afternoon, the streets were filled with Ndebele women with shaven heads and rings of bead and copper jangling on their necks and arms. Beside them, naked children played with colored stones in the dusty street, or played hide-and-seek under the huge brightly colored blankets their mothers wore.

He drove slowly through the narrow, busy street and turned onto a road that led up a slight incline to a residential area higher than the rest of the little city. There were wealthy blacks in South Africa, too, traders and merchants. Some of them lived here, including the prime minister of Athatsawana, Chief Kaiser Bophusta Ran.

The street was lined on both sides by sidewalks and clay walls covered in bright geometric designs. The peaks of the round thatched roofs of the big houses were visible over the walls. The prime minister's house, in African style like the rest of them, was easy to spot. The flag of Athatsawana flew by the gates, and guards with submachine guns patrolled the streets to protect the man—considered a collaborator and traitor by the guerrillas and his own people.

Paul pulled his car over and was quickly waved through into the first courtyard. Leaving the Ferrari, he walked through the large carved wooden doorway of the main house, where a servant greeted him.

"Athustra," Paul said.

The servant nodded and disappeared wordlessly. The large round room of the main house was lit only by light streaming in the door and small oil lamps set on elegant wooden tables around the sides of the room. At the back, a wooden platform with cushions offered a place to sit. There was nothing else. African homes were famous for their simplicity.

A moment later the servant reappeared and led him through a wide doorway into another round room with a high thatched ceiling. They passed through into another courtyard behind the house where a small fountain burbled in a little pool of water. Plants grew in a rock garden along the walls.

A young African woman stood by the little pool. Like other Ndebele women, she wore many rings on her neck, wrists and legs. Hers were of silver and gold. Her black hair was coiled tightly on top of her head, and woven with colored beads. She wore a thin African printed cloth around her body, forcefully outlining her narrow waist and full breasts. Her brown skin was burnished from the hot sun of the veldts. She watched him enter the courtyard, the impassive expression on her face carefully masking anything she felt.

"Athustra," the servant said, bowing.

"Leave us alone," the woman commanded.

The servant bowed again and backed out of the courtyard into the darkness of the house.

Alone, the white man and the black woman stared at each other without speaking.

"Paul," she said suddenly, her face relaxing into relief. She ran across the distance that separated them and flung herself into his arms.

He grabbed her warm body and held her tightly in his arms, breathing her in as if she were a fragrant flower.

He let go, and pushed her away.

"What's the matter, Paul?" she asked, worried by the expression on his face.

He drew a small leather sack from his pocket and emptied it into his hands. His palm filled with stones like soapy glass the size of marbles. Raw diamonds.

"From Peter today?" the African woman asked.

Paul nodded. "Half of what he brought out. Then they killed him."

She looked at her lover, speechless with shock.

"He's dead," Paul said harshly. "Peter is dead. Mthuli must have been captured and made to talk."

"Then you..."

"I'm all right," Paul said emphatically. "I'm white and my father's one of the wealthiest men in South Africa. But it means the whole operation is at an end. They killed our people who took the diamonds into Mozambique. And now they've killed the man who got the diamonds for us from the mines."

Agitated by the crisis, he looked down and shook the diamonds in his hand.

"That's one of the problems with cell organization," he continued. "They closed in at both ends. Now we're isolated. We don't know anyone else to go to."

Athustra walked to him and touched his arms. "I know one other," she said calmly.

"Where?" The rough question betrayed Paul's discouragement.

"In Soweto. I have to go there. My father has imprisoned the resistance here in Athatsawana. I'll go tonight, and I'll give you instructions to get there, too.

It's the house of a man named Samora. He is a witch doctor. I am very worried about you."

"I'll be all right."

"I love you, Paul." She buried her face in his chest.

"It's illegal for a black woman to love a white man," he said, shaking his head.

"I don't care. I love you, anyway. They cannot outlaw love."

He wrapped his arms tightly around her again, as if she were the one thing he could hang on to for life and safety. "But they have, my dear," he told her.

"So then we must be outlaws."

"We are." He kissed her forehead lightly. "We are."

WHEN MAJOR SNIDER RETURNED from dinner, Mthuli was lying on the shiny tile floor of his office. He was no longer alive.

Johann, a big burly man whose specialty ensured his steady work in the state security apparatus, sat carelessly in an iron chair, wiping his hands on a damp cloth and sponging spatters of blood off his shirt.

Major Snider glanced quickly at the body as he stepped over it and sat at his desk. He opened the right-hand drawer and pulled out the pad of forms headed "Death Report."

"So who's moving the diamonds?" he asked Johann, picking up his pen.

"Sure you want to know?"

"Sure I'm sure," he said shortly as he filled out the dead man's name and number.

"Paul Krudd." Johann stood up and looked over Snider's shoulder at the report. The major's pen hovered over the line headed "Cause of Death," temporarily frozen.

"You're absolutely sure?"

Johann nodded. "That's what he said," inclining his head toward the body on the floor. "And they don't lie when I ask the questions."

Major Snider's pen landed. He wrote "Suicide" on the line.

"You surprised?" Johann asked.

"I've suspected."

Johann leaned over the desk and tapped the form with his thick finger. "The last one was suicide, too," he cautioned.

"Quite right." Major Snider crumpled the paper into a ball and tore another sheet off the pad. "Any suggestions?"

Johann shrugged and moved away from the desk, stepping over the corpse on his way to the door.

"Died in a scuffle?"

"Good idea," said Major Snider, and he filled in the appropriate space.

12

Geoff Bishop pushed through the frosted glass doors into the hotel's fitness center. Like most hotel gyms, it was nearly deserted. Alex Nanos was lifting weights and proudly showing a pretty young woman his muscles. A black caretaker carefully skimmed the surface of the swimming pool.

Nanos lowered the barbell into the bench support as Bishop came nearer. The pilot nodded to the woman and introduced himself.

"You're from the airplane, aren't you?" he asked, recognizing the flight attendant.

"That's right. My name's Dianne. Are you a pilot?"

"When I have something to fly," he said with a laugh.

"What are you doing back so soon?" Nanos asked gruffly, sitting up on the bench.

"I'm tempted to ask you the same thing. I went to the airport office of the Bureau of State Security as instructed and asked them about the helicopter they supposedly had waiting for us. They said, 'helicopter?' as if they'd never heard of the invention."

"So no chopper?"

Bishop pulled some car keys from his pocket. "Nope. They claimed that their instructions were to give me a four-wheel-drive Land Rover. A great vehicle, but it doesn't fly. And I thought you and Lee were meeting Major Snider to go over security arrangements.''

''We were. He canceled,'' Nanos said, standing up with his back to Geoff Bishop.

''Come on over here, Dianne. Let me show you how I keep my abs in shape.''

Bishop went into the change room and slipped into his bathing suit. When he returned to the workout room the flight attendant had gone and Alex was doing sit-ups.

''Where'd your friend go?'' Bishop asked innocently.

Nanos continued his sit-ups, ignoring the question. He looked sullen and angry.

''What's the matter, Alex?'' Bishop said finally with a sense of frustration. ''Sometimes you're a decent guy and sometimes you treat me like I'm bad news.''

''Sometimes, man, you are bad news.''

''What's eating you?''

The Greek abruptly stopped exercising and jumped to his feet to confront the Canadian face-to-face. ''Man, I saw you cruise Dianne when you walked in here.''

Bishop rolled his eyes. ''Alex, you're imagining—''

''Don't fucking tell me I'm making it up, man!'' Nanos jumped at Bishop, his fist raised and his face red with fury. Bishop backed off, his hands out protectively, trying to calm the mad Greek. At the same time he slowly flexed, prepared to spring into action if he had to.

Nanos wasn't finished. ''Man, you want to move in on her just like you moved in on Lee Hatton.''

Geoff Bishop was speechless. He and Hatton were supposed to be a secret item.

"Yeah, that's right, man. I know. Everyone knows. But don't think I'm going to let you move in on this one." He stalked away toward the door of the fitness room.

"Alex, you're jealous." Bishop was too stunned by the Greek's overly active imagination to say anything else.

Nanos turned back to look at Bishop. He pointed his finger as if he meant business. "Just remember, Bishop. Me and the other guys have been working as a team for a while. You're the new boy. So watch whose territory you're moving in on. Or sometime in the heat of battle you might not have all the friends you need."

"Is that a threat, Alex?"

"A warning, buddy."

Just then the glass door parted and Barrabas strode into the room in sweat pants and a T-shirt. He carried a rolled newspaper.

"Anything the matter?" he asked, sensing the tense atmosphere between the two men.

"Uh-uh," Nanos said quickly, looking at Bishop. "Everything's just fine."

"What happened this afternoon?" the colonel asked, referring to their assignments.

They told him about their lack of success. Barrabas picked up a fifteen-pound dumbbell and almost threw it against a wall.

"Looks like you didn't get much done, either," Bishop commented.

Without another word to either of them, Nanos turned around and pushed through the glass doors, leaving Barrabas and his pilot alone.

"What's the matter?" Barrabas asked.

"Nothing," Bishop said, trying to make it sound innocent. He picked up a dumbbell and started doing curls with it.

Barrabas threw down the one he was holding and stared at Geoff Bishop. The colonel was great at fighting wars, but dealing with personality clashes was out of his league. The easy solution was to tell one or both of the men they were through, fired, finished, take their problems somewhere else. But aside from the fact that Barrabas didn't take the easy way out of anything, both men were damned good soldiers and important members of the team.

"What do you figure's going on?" Bishop asked, changing the subject. "From the sounds of it, two no-shows on the part of Krudd and Snider, and a Land Rover instead of a helicopter sounds more like a conspiracy than coincidence."

"Damned right it does," Barrabas said. He was piling additional weights onto the barbell Nanos had just finished with. "We're being set up."

"In other words they're telling us to get lost."

"Very clearly." He pushed himself under the weight and gripped it with both hands.

"You have any ideas what to do next?"

"Press about a hundred of these until I'm too exhausted to be pissed off."

Bishop laughed. "And then?"

"Have you seen today's headlines?"

"No." Bishop picked up the newspaper that Barrabas had thrown onto the floor. The banner headline screamed "Toto takes refuge—Aides outraged." A quick skim of the first few paragraphs told him that the famous bishop had taken up residence at the Krudd estate. Black organizations were furious, calling for an explanation. The famous bishop promised a news conference at the estate that evening.

"I think the four of us should pay Wilhelm Krudd a visit at his home this evening," Barrabas told him.

Bishop walked to the edge of the pool and stood poised for a shallow dive. Barrabas started pressing.

"Geoff!"

The Canadian pilot looked at his leader. Barrabas had paused, holding the weight straight up, his elbows locked, his face knotted with tension from the load.

"If Nanos gives you static, I want to know."

"Sure, Colonel. No static."

"Good." Barrabas lowered the weight slowly and pressed again, grunting the air out of his lungs. He held the bar high again. "I don't like problems," he said.

Bishop could feel himself trembling with anger at the stupid chip the Greek was carrying around on his shoulder. Both shoulders. Chip, hell. The Greek was carrying a fucking motherlode.

He dived in the pool and butterfly-stroked up and down the length of it until he was too exhausted to go on.

WHEN PAUL KRUDD DROVE UP to the family estate in Parktown, it was almost dark. The sun dipped under the horizon and the deep gray sky faded into a thin line of orange and white in the far west. The trees and gardens of Parktown exuded a mysterious green so dark it was almost colorless. The air had cooled a little, and a light wind from the veldt tossed the topmost leaves in the high branches of the African trees. The evening was pregnant with dark expectation, as if the oncoming night knew what was about to happen.

The spacious driveway in front of the big front doors was clogged with equipment vans and floodlit with television lights.

Paul cursed and slammed the steering wheel. He'd completely forgotten about the press conference for Bishop Toto. It was weird enough for the bishop to be staying as a guest of his father's, anyway. But there were some things about South African politics he couldn't penetrate.

He tripped up the steps, skipping over the thick rubber-coated cables strung like burned spaghetti out the front doors and across the drive to the vans. The night was blue with the haze of the television lights. Smiling, wide-eyed script assistants milled among scowling technicians.

The servant at the door greeted him happily. The foyer under the two-ton chandelier was jammed with people jostling for position among the cameras, cables and cops. At least half the people there had fire-power of some kind or another.

Bishop Toto was seated at a long table on the far side of the hall, illuminated by the intense white light from the portable spots around the room. On his left, Wilhelm Krudd smiled sincerely at the folks out there in television land. On the bishop's right, one of his aides watched his leader speak with a skeptical lift of the eyebrow. The bishop was making a lot of waves with his so-called outreach to South Africa's white population.

Richard Krudd walked casually over to his younger brother.

"I've heard what happened at the mine today, Paul."

"You don't sound too upset about it," Paul said as the two brothers circled slowly around the back of the crowd.

"Why should I be?"

"Maybe because a man was killed?" Paul suggested.

"He was a thief. A terrorist and a criminal. He deserved to die. The electric fence only saved the executioner some work."

"I see," Paul said coldly.

"Don't get too upset about it," Richard told him.

"I won't," Paul promised. In the crowd he could make out Bishop Bloemvaal, Henry Miller and Pieter van den Boos. All the men who went to those secret gatherings his father hosted were present. He had wanted to know for some time what went on behind the closed doors of the study. Tonight he was prepared for it.

"One of father's little meetings tonight?" he asked his brother.

Richard looked slightly surprised. "Yes, actually. How did you know?"

"All the members of the club are here. What do you do in there, anyway?" He looked at his brother innocently.

Richard stammered nervously, trying to think of a fast answer. "Oh, mostly discuss charity things. Fund raising. Things such as that."

"Oh." Paul nodded as if he understood. "Just a group of philanthropists sitting down to decide what to do with their disposable incomes."

"Yes, exactly."

At the table, Wilhelm Krudd was announcing the end of the press conference. He raised his hands adamantly to insist over the protests of the press that there would be no more questions.

Almost immediately technicians began running about the foyer snapping off the spotlights and coiling their cables. Bishop Toto was shaking hands with several aides and black colleagues and preparing to leave the room. Wilhelm Krudd sauntered over to his two sons.

"Terrible what happened at the mine today," he told Paul. "Dreadful thing. God knows how many diamonds were lost before the terrorist was smoked out."

"True," Paul said dully, in hopeless agreement. For a moment he felt tired of the game he was playing and wanted to rip off the mask, tell them what he was doing and the truth about their racism. Instead he nodded, smiled, agreed and went for another roll of the dice.

"Richard, we'll be meeting immediately in the study, if you care to join us. Paul—" he turned to his younger son "—I'm expecting this man Barrabas and his people at the house this evening. I expect they'll be a little upset. Certain people in the American government insisted that we have observers to oversee the security arrangements for Bishop Toto's consecration tomorrow. We agreed and since their arrival here, we've made it as difficult as possible for them to do their job. That's the real reason I was unable to go to the mine today." Krudd spoke with a satisfied smile spreading across his face. "We don't need these foreigners snooping around South African internal matters. If they come while we're in the study, I'll rely on you to keep them calm and entertained."

Paul stiffened at the unwelcome assignment.

"I know it's unpleasant," his father said understandingly. "But it's important. Richard?" He beckoned, and father and elder son left for their meeting.

The foyer had already been cleared of the reporters and technicians. A few security officers stood around as servants busily cleaned up the coffee cups and ashtrays and put the furnishings back in place.

Paul walked quickly to the stairs that spiraled to the second floor, passing the room where coffee tables had been set up for the press conference.

Bishop Toto was alone in the room. Paul stopped and pulled himself back behind some curtains in the doorway to watch.

Thinking himself unobserved, the black bishop had removed a set of false teeth. He greedily shoved a handful of sugar cubes into his mouth and sucked on them.

Paul was perplexed by the man's behavior. He was an internationally famous figure, a renowned Christian theologian, one of the staunchest of the moderate black leaders working against apartheid in South Africa, and as of tomorrow he would be bishop of Johannesburg. But right now he was acting like a simple, hungry laborer from an impoverished homeland. There was something very unbishoplike about Toto in his private moments.

Paul shook his head in disbelief and silently ran up the stairs two at a time.

He entered a guest bedroom at the back of the great house and quietly closed and locked the door behind him. He took off his shoes. It was dark, except for a gray glow from outside the house. He tiptoed over the polished wood floor to the center of the room, squatted and carefully rolled up a small Indian rug. A tiny hole, barely a quarter of an inch in diameter, had been drilled into one of the planks. He put his eye to it and looked straight down between the layers of floor to the study directly below.

This was an example of good old American know-how. All his father's expensive security sensors were ineffective against a simple spy hole Paul had secretly drilled into the ceiling a day earlier. By lying flat on his stomach and pushing himself slowly around in a circle he had a clear view of all the conspirators below. Most important, their conversation was clearly audible.

They were just taking their seats. Bishop Bloemvaal, the short fat little primate of the white Afrikaner church, Henry Miller, the frail nervous director of the Institute for Separate Development Studies, Pieter van den Boos, the thin, spidery gold mine owner, Wilhelm Krudd, smug and satisfied as ever, and his detestable brother, Richard. The saviors of the white race.

His father cleared his throat and the meeting of the Inner Circle was called to order.

"It's working," Krudd said. "The press conference tonight was a tremendous success." His voice rang with satisfaction.

Van den Boos smiled thinly, almost in spite of himself. "I must say, Sidney really has done an excellent job. The man he found to play Bishop Toto is excellent. No one suspects he's an impostor at all. I had my doubts it was possible. But I really have to give Sidney credit."

The telephone in the study beeped softly. Krudd answered and spoke briefly. He hung up. "You can congratulate Major Snider in person. He's just arrived at the gates and is on his way in."

"But can we be absolutely sure the plan will work tomorrow?" Miller asked anxiously, blinking rapidly behind his thick glasses.

Krudd and van den Boos exchanged glances.

"I think so," Krudd said.

"Yes, Snider's work has been quite efficient on all counts," van den Boos commented. "Our impostor has already created a great deal of tension and suspense in his statements giving many concessions to the government. Already, the major black organizations are upset. The radicals will almost certainly start a riot."

"Besides," Richard Krudd interjected smugly, "the security forces will have their own agents scattered through the crowd."

As he was speaking, the door to the study opened and Major Snider walked in. From his ceiling peephole, Paul could not see the man standing by the door. But he recognized the chilling voice.

"Not only will my agents ensure a major riot, they will also see to it that if the rioters do not kill Toto, they will."

He strode to the remaining armchair and threw himself down in it. He looked relaxed and comfortable.

"Congratulations, Major," said van den Boos. "You've done an excellent job."

"But do tell us, I am so curious," Bloemvaal began, "where the real Bishop Toto is and what will you do to him."

"Right now he's alive and in a secret place. He's our insurance policy as long as he's alive. When the impostor dies tomorrow, he will be executed."

Paul pulled his head back from the peephole, reeling as the full import of the assassination plan hit him.

It was incredible. He felt himself trembling uncontrollably with fear, but forced himself to listen and watch again.

"There is one other matter to discuss," Major Snider continued. He ran his fingers absentmindedly along the edge of the side table, without looking at the others.

"Ah, yes," said Wilhelm Krudd. "The matter of the diamonds. That was excellent work today, Sidney. Excellent."

"A pity the Zulu was killed so soon," van den Boos said. "He might have provided information."

"We no longer need information," Major Snider told them, looking up for the first time. His expression was quite grim. "We have all the information we require."

"What do you mean?" Richard Krudd asked. "Doesn't the death of this miner end the investigation?"

"Perhaps you gentlemen forget that it is impossible for a Bantu worker to smuggle the diamonds out of the compound. So even though the worker who was killed today brought the diamonds from the mine to the surface..."

"He still needed someone to take the diamonds out of the compound!" van den Boos crowed, his logic triumphant.

"Then who is this connection?" Wilhelm Krudd asked, his voice steady, chin up.

Snider paused and looked from face to face before dropping the bomb.

"Your son. Paul."

The room was silent. All eyes were riveted on Wilhelm Krudd.

"You are absolutely sure?" the industrialist asked slowly, betraying no emotion.

"It was information we received during an interrogation. Since then my investigators examined your son's visits to the mines. They correspond exactly with all known shipments that arrived in Mozambique and Amsterdam. There can be no doubt." Snider eyed Krudd. "It looks as if America was a bad influence on him."

"Yes, of course. That explains why he's so irritable whenever..." Richard Krudd began, his enthusiasm tinged with evident malice.

"Shut up!" Wilhelm snapped at his eldest son. He tapped his fingers nervously on the arm of the chesterfield. "He's in the house now. You can arrange for it to be blamed on terrorists."

"Arrange what?" Snider asked.

"His murder."

"You mean..."

"Yes! Kill him! Now! I want him dead!"

13

Nile Barrabas and the SOBs arrived at the gates of the Krudd estate in the Land Rover with Geoff Bishop at the wheel of what he called his South African helicopter. Barrabas stepped out and handed their papers to the stone-faced guard with the FN-FAL rifle. The guard scanned the photographs, then the faces of the mercs. They returned his efficient gaze with cold, steady stares.

"We're expected this evening," Barrabas told him firmly. The guard looked down the list on his clipboard.

"You're the Americans," he said. "Right. I'll call the house."

He went to the intercom set in the stone wall of the guard hut and pressed the buzzer. While he waited for the house to answer, he motioned to two other guards to open the steel gates wide enough to allow the Land Rover through. Barrabas walked around to get back in.

Bishop eased off the brake and the Land Rover rolled forward. Suddenly, from the hillside above, a single shot punctured the night. Then there was a chatter-burst of automatic-rifle fire and the sound of a car engine roaring to life.

The security guards looked at their leader for instructions. He pressed rapidly on the intercom buzzer to get the attention of his superior, shouting rapidly into the transmitter. He wasn't getting a response.

"Shut the gates!" he yelled, waving his arms madly.

The two guards began to push them closed across the double driveway.

The Land Rover was in the way.

The guards waved their rifles in the air and yelled at the mercs to back out.

"Pull inside," Barrabas snapped at Bishop.

The Canadian turned the wheel sharply and drove ahead, clearing the entrance. One guard ran in front to block further progress. The automatic rifle he aimed at the front windshield guaranteed it.

The other guard and the commander began to push the heavy gates closed.

At the top of the driveway headlights appeared. They came fast down the hill. The high beams bathed the Land Rover and the security men in their glow, and the car came faster, aiming for the guard in front of the Rover.

"He's going to hit us head-on," Bishop mumbled, driving the gear into forward and letting off the clutch. The guard in front of them figured it out fast. He was going to be squashed between the bumpers of the two cars when they crashed. He panicked and threw himself off the road with a scream of terror.

Bishop pressed hard on the gas and veered sharply right, pulling the Land Rover off the driveway into the garden. The car coming at them, the small red Ferrari that belonged to Paul Krudd, missed them by inches. The escaping car swerved, its tires screaming sharply and the rear end fishtailing as the driver aimed for the narrow opening between the two gates.

The two security men leaped for their lives. One didn't make it. The Ferrari hit him. The man bounced into the air like a rubber ball and came down on the hood.

But the Ferrari didn't stop. The guard sailed over the sleek aerodynamically designed windshield and over the roof. The flailing body landed with a crumpled thud in the driveway, the head split open on the asphalt like a ripe melon.

The commander recovered from his leap and rolled over onto his knees, ripping a handgun from his holster.

The red Ferrari veered sharply onto the street, slowing slightly, then picking up speed again as the driver brought it out of another fishtail. The guard fired after the escaping car, but the Ferrari vanished with a roar from its precision engine down the long residential street.

The mercs jumped from the Land Rover and rushed to the wounded men. More cars poured down the driveway from the hilltop mansion, then braked abruptly at the gates.

Major Snider jumped from the lead car, yelling frantically.

"Who opened the goddamned gates?" He saw the Americans. "This time you've interfered once too often," he said, his rage mounting. "Clear the road!"

Lee Hatton leaned over the body of the guard who had been hit by the Ferrari, checking his pulse.

"He's dead," she said.

"You didn't have to tell me." Barrabas could see the guy's brains seeping onto the road from the back of his head.

Snider and two of his men grabbed the dead man by his arms and legs and swung the body into the gardens, blood and brain matter flying across the asphalt.

"What the hell's..." Barrabas began.

Snider shot him a look of absolute hatred. "They tried to assassinate Bishop Toto, and they've taken Paul Krudd hostage. And you're responsible for their getaway." He pointed his finger at the American colonel.

Before Barrabas could respond, the man from BOSS and his men jumped into their car and tore past them through the gates.

Nanos was helping a security guard out of the bushes and onto the road. The man had hurt his leg badly during his leap from certain death. Bishop stood by the guardhouse.

"Is there a police radio in there?" Barrabas demanded from the security officer who was slipping his gun back into his holster. The man nodded slowly.

"Geoff, monitor it. Find out where they're going."

Another car, Wilhelm Krudd's Rolls-Royce, came over the crest of the hill, the silver hood ornament winking against the lights along the wall of the estate. The car slowed at the entrance and the diamond industrialist stuck his worried head out of the driver's window.

Barrabas walked over to him. "Maybe you can tell me what the hell is going on," he said.

"Terrorists. Two of them. Somehow they got in and tried to kill the bishop. Major Snider and my guards stopped them but they fled in my son's sports car. And they've taken Paul hostage."

"Didn't look like terrorists in that car to me," Barrabas said slowly, watching the man's face.

"What do you mean?" Krudd asked fiercely.

"Well, it went by awfully fast," Barrabas said slowly. "But it looked to me like your son Paul was driving. And he was alone."

"You're mistaken," Wilhelm Krudd said firmly. "It was obviously going too fast for you to see clearly."

"I see." Barrabas nodded doubtfully. "They must have been pretty small terrorists to squeeze into that little car."

Krudd opened his mouth to respond but thought better of it. He looked indignant.

"Are you calling me a liar?" Krudd finally said.

"Yeah, I guess I am," Barrabas replied.

Just then Geoff Bishop came from the guard booth. "Colonel, the Ferrari has been reported leaving Johannesburg. Apparently it's creating a lot of havoc. It's faster than the police cars that are chasing it and it's already battered its way through two roadblocks. It's headed out the Main Reef Road now."

Krudd listened intently. Barrabas looked at him.

"Soweto!" Krudd said to himself. He rolled up his window and drove the Rolls out of the driveway onto the street, leaving the Americans behind.

"Nanos! Hatton!" Barrabas turned to give orders. But the SOBs were already with him. Nanos pulled open the back doors of the Land Rover and lifted the heavy metal lid on the spare-tire compartment. Lee hauled out the small Uzi submachine guns. The Uzis had been preferred for this assignment. Their light weight and small size made them the weapon of choice for urban warfare of any kind.

The mercs lifted their hardware. "Let's go!" Barrabas snapped, pacing briskly toward the front seat of the Land Rover.

"Soweto?" Geoff Bishop asked, climbing in behind the wheel.

"That's where the action is."

"What are we going to do when we get there?" Hatton asked from the back seat.

"Get some answers," Barrabas replied.

CLAUDE HAYES WALKED QUICKLY down the steps of the Johannesburg railway station, pushing through the crowds in the narrow passageways and going in the opposite direction of the signs that read White Only. There was a separate station platform for the thousands of black Africans who, at night, were forced to leave Johannesburg. The black curfew time was approaching. Most of the two hundred thousand daily workers had already gone from the white city. Those who were left walked quickly up the steps to the black platform, fearful of violating their work permits.

After the death of the Zulu miner, Hayes had gone to his foreman begging for permission to travel to Soweto, claiming his aging mother's imminent death as his reason. The foreman had refused to give him the pass he required to get past the guards at the gates of the mine complex. Finally the American merc had slipped some "chocolate" across the table. "Chocolate" was the Bantu slang for the brown twenty-rand notes they were paid with. The mine foreman looked at the notes and quietly placed his hand over them. The money disappeared from the table and was quickly replaced by the needed permit. Hayes hitched a ride with one of the trucks that brought food supplies to the compound, arriving in Pretoria in the late afternoon. Two hours later he was in Johannesburg, hurrying through the crowds of black workers leaving the city.

Men and women squeezed past him down the narrow steps, their coats buttoned tightly and their elbows close to their sides to protect themselves from pickpockets and robbery. Samora had warned Hayes about the electric trains before he started at the mines.

Roaming gangs of African bullyboys wearing school uniforms used the politically organized boycott of government-controlled schools to play hooky and terrorize passengers on the trains. And the country that had the most sophisticated secret police surveillance of its own citizens in the world was apparently powerless to do anything about it.

On the underground platform, conductors yelled above the heads of the milling crowd. People squeezed through the open doors into the waiting cars. Guards positioned themselves at regular intervals outside the locked entrances to the first-class cars where prosperous blacks sat in comfort reading their newspapers.

The rest of the workers jammed into the third-class cars, up to five hundred in each one, until there was barely room to breathe, and each traveler was frozen into position by the crush of people.

Finally the doors to the wagon closed, the lights dimmed slightly and the electric current buzzed through the car. The train pulled forward on its tracks and left the station. The passengers relaxed in the steady rhythm of the thirty-five-minute ride to the New Canada junction in Soweto.

No sooner had the train pulled out of the underground tunnel with the lights of Johannesburg's office towers growing smaller behind them than the smell of marijuana and glue floated through the hot airless car. People turned away from it, their faces lined with worry. The smells signaled the presence of one of the robber gangs, and danger.

There was movement at the far end of the car and a group of big black men, their faces scarred, and wearing blankets that were traditionally part of the Xhosa clothing, elbowed their way through the passengers who were more than willing to let them pass.

They carried short sharpened sticks. These were the "Russians," as the people of Soweto had nicknamed them—vigilante groups of traditional African men who patrolled the black townships and trains to protect their fellow blacks where the forces of South African authority could not, or would not. They caught their own criminals, tried them in their own courts and carried out their own judgments. No one interfered. Everyone knew better.

When the Russians reached the end of the car, they stood threateningly before a group of three teenage boys in school uniforms. The smell of marijuana and glue remained, but the joints and glue had disappeared.

The schoolboys looked innocent.

But they weren't.

The Russians grabbed them as the other passengers pushed out of the immediate area. The crowd turned away, not wanting to watch. The boys were quickly shoved against the wall. One protested and a heavy stick was slammed across his back. He shut up.

Two other men started to frisk the boys, removing sharpened bicycle spokes and crude tin knives from the pockets of their pants and blazers.

Then the punishment began.

Hayes squeezed his eyes closed and turned away, like the other passengers. There was nothing pleasant to hear in the sounds of thuds and groans as the air was knocked from their bodies and fists smacked into their faces. This was the degradation forced on black Africans by a white slave state. Made to protect themselves from the forces of disorder, they used methods that were primitive and brutal. It was the best they could do in the primitive and brutal society they were forced to live in.

Mercifully the train pulled into the elevated platform at the New Canada junction. The vigilantes were the first to leave, pushing their prisoners ahead of them.

The air was filled with the screams of distant sirens, and from the elevated station Hayes could see the flashing cherry tops of police cars driving along the adjacent highway at fast speeds. A roadblock had been set up at the entrance to the township. Beyond, flames shot from one of the wooden buildings on a nearby street. Worry flickered like firelight across the faces of the other travelers.

There was too much activity for just a house on fire.

And the long convoy of two-ton army trucks and personnel carriers indicated something major was happening.

As the Russians were hustling their captives into an old pickup truck parked by the curb, Hayes called to one of them and walked over. The big Xhosa man eyed him with suspicion.

Hayes flipped open his passbook with the travel permit. "The police have come. I'm frightened," he said deferentially.

The biggest of them, a man with long knife scars running like the ravines of dried rivers down each side of his face, examined Hayes's papers closely.

"No worry," he said. He smiled a little and peered closely at the travel permit. "Samora does good work." He reached into the truck and handed Hayes a short club with a round knob on the end, like the one Nkono had used in their earlier fight.

"Good luck," the Xhosa told him. He turned back to the business of the delinquent teenagers.

Claude Hayes faded into the troubled night.

14

Three roadblocks later, Barrabas and his soldiers pulled up in front of the guard post that marked the permanently manned entrance to the black township of Soweto. The night was loud with the sharp shouts of police and cut by the flashing red lights on their vehicles. A stream of army trucks had pulled over along the shoulders of the road, and riot-equipped soldiers wearing helmets and carrying plastic shields, leather truncheons and rifles hopped out and assembled in even rows. More trucks continued to arrive. Across the flat, uninhabited veldt on the Johannesburg side of the township line, similar activity could be seen at another highway in the distance. Soweto was being closed off and surrounded. On the other side of the guard post a tow truck pulled a red Ferrari toward them. It was empty. The windshield was smashed, the hood and sides crumpled and torn. As it went through the flickering lights, Barrabas could see that the driver's seat was wet with blood.

Major Snider was surrounded by a group of officers and plain clothes security men not far from the roadblock. He saw Barrabas as the big white-haired man walked over to him. The American warrior wanted to wipe the contemptuous look off Snider's face with a fist.

"This is your doing, Colonel Barrabas," Snider said loudly over the roar of the assault on Soweto. "This is what happens when you bleeding-heart Yankees interfere in South African affairs. You and your people can just bloody well turn around and get out of here!"

Barrabas didn't even think about it. He just reached out his long arm and grabbed Snider by the neck of his shirt, his big hand tightening on the fabric. He twisted to choke the man from BOSS, and lifted him just enough for Snider to feel his weight coming off the ground.

The men around him reached for their guns. Two of them jumped forward and grabbed the American.

"Hold it!" Bishop shouted from the background. The security men turned to see him standing ten feet away with Nanos and Lee Hatton. Their Uzis were raised just enough to let the soldiers know they meant business.

"Stalemate, Snider. Tell your goons to relax."

Snider looked into Barrabas's eyes, and what he saw there made him consider.

"Back off, men," he muttered tightly. "Back off!"

His men lowered their guns and took their hands off Barrabas's arms. Barrabas lowered Snider just slightly, as a concession, but kept his hand gripped tightly on the man's collar.

Barrabas spoke slowly through gritted teeth.

"Snider, you might be a big-time cop here. And my instructions are to cooperate with you and your people. But I am sick of your crap, and I'm sick of Krudd's crap. And I'm warning you that if you don't cooperate beginning now, terrible things are going to start to happen. Now I want to know what the hell is going on."

He let go of Snider's neck and the man fell back a step or two, bringing his hand up to his collar. His eyes glowed with hatred for Barrabas and everything the American stood for.

"I'm a civilized man, Colonal Barrabas. And this is a civilized country."

"You could have fooled me."

"Okay." Snider brushed his shirt where Barrabas's hands had touched it. A little smile played on his lips. "You want to see the results of what you've done. Go ahead." He motioned with his head toward the streets of Soweto. A column of troops was marching into the township, the steady even beat of their heavy heels drumming on the pavement. The flickering red cherry lights and the long swoops of brilliant spots bathed over the youthful white faces of the South African storm troopers. Their eyes were fixed hypnotically ahead of them, and they marched past in four long even lines at a steady pace.

"You have my permission. My men will leave you alone. Go ahead." Snider said it as if it was a dare.

"Where's Paul Krudd?"

"The terrorists got him," Snider said defiantly. "We found the car, but Paul's gone. We'll look until we find him. In there." He jerked his thumb toward Soweto. "House by house."

An ugly sound broke the night in two, the sound of truncheons thudding heavily on closed wooden doors, first one, then a second, a third, fourth, fifth, sixth until it came like a deafening drumbeat followed by the shouts of soldiers and the splintering and smashing of unyielding doors being forced open.

The screams began. First the voices of women in terror, then the cries of children and babies, and finally of men in pain stretched down from the Soweto streets to the roadblock. The cries of the people mingled with the hard snap of marching boots. The soldiers ran in parties, crying savagely like frenzied beasts, door to door, house to house, family to family.

Barrabas turned to the SOBs. "Let's get the hell out of here!" he shouted above the madness. The mercenaries stared at the South African police. Their revulsion was apparent in the flickering lights. Barrabas ran for the Land Rover and they followed.

"Where to?" Bishop asked, climbing behind the wheel.

"Right into the middle of it," the colonel told him.

They drove past the security cars and the long line of empty army trucks that lined the road, past the first houses on the edge of Soweto where women and children stood weeping and covered their eyes in terror. A dozen men were spread-eagled on the ground as soldiers frisked them roughly, jerked their hands behind their backs, handcuffed them and led them away.

They pulled over and let a honking jeep carrying officers speed by. Another long line of troops marched evenly past, penetrating deeper and deeper into Soweto. More women ran with their children into the open door of a little church where a black minister stood guard over his flock. Security forces picked the men from the throngs of fleeing Africans and quarantined them in a growing crowd surrounded by guards with submachine guns. Smaller groups were pulled aside and searched.

Geoff Bishop pulled the Land Rover over again when another long convoy pushed up behind them. This time it was paddy wagons.

"We'll get out here and walk," Barrabas said.

The mercs grabbed their rifles and left the four-wheel. A building farther down the road had caught fire, greedy flames gnawing at the roof and licking the night sky. And still the sounds of soldiers running, the breaking and splintering of doors and windows continued.

The SOBs started walking.

At the end of the street, where a long, flat-roofed building that might have been a school sat on an open lot, a crowd had gathered. Now the bullyboys and the "Russians" were side by side, united against their common enemy. There were already hundreds of them, and hundreds more poured down from side streets, chanting and yelling at the soldiers. Rocks began to fly. Many of the black youths carried shields of corrugated iron and short, knobbed wooden sticks. They started banging on the iron shields. The racket was deafening.

The soldiers lined the streets waiting for orders. The visors of their helmets were down and their Plexiglas shields up. Armored vehicles poured down the road and took up places opposite the growing crowd of protestors.

Rocks, bottles and pieces of glass flew in a hailstorm of fury from the black mob.

For their own protection from the deadly rain, the mercs ducked behind a paddy wagon. Rocks hit the windows and shattered them.

The hard beating of the clubs on iron shields and the chanting of the rioters was suddenly punctuated by the soft popping and muzzle-flashing from the soldiers' rifles.

Tear gas.

The canisters fell in front of the first line of demonstrators, spewing their smoky contents into low clouds. Caught by the winds, the gas swirled upward as if indecisive about which direction to take. The gray clouds mushroomed over the streets and the front line pushed back. Some panicked and ran. The rain of rocks abated. The riot troops, with their gas masks firmly over their faces, began to march forward, their rifles raised high.

An officer shouted an order and dozens of rifles in the front line of troops flared. Bird shot blammed into the throng of protesters. People fell, their iron shields clattering to the pavement underneath them. The mob turned and fled, people running in all directions. Led by the armored vehicles, the troops marched on, stepping neatly over the bodies of the people they had just cut down.

"This way!" Barrabas shouted to his soldiers. He led them in a breathless run down a narrow deserted alleyway on the troops' side of the battle zone, then cut through a junk-filled backyard to the street where hundreds of demonstrators ran. Panic and anger were written across their faces like words engraved in stone. The American warriors stopped abruptly by a house and pressed against it.

"If we go out there, we'll be just more white men with guns," Barrabas said.

The mob of fleeing Africans suddenly stopped running and turned to fight back, hurling more rocks and bottles at the pursuing South African troops. There was another horrible volley of rifle shots. People on the street screamed and fell as pools of blood flowed from underneath their crumpled bodies.

The rest turned to run again, the troops fast on their heels. Blacks tripped and stumbled over one another in their haste to get away. The South African troops waded in among the helpless prey, truncheons raised high, cracking the heads of their victims.

"Let's go," Barrabas told his soldiers. "I want to stay ahead of the police lines." He led them quickly back into the alley and farther into Soweto. The sounds of battle grew a little fainter. Dogs barked in the backyards of the small brick houses.

In the spaces between the buildings, they could see the Soweto residents regrouping on the street. The alley ended in a sharp turn, which led to a broad intersection. There, the battle lines had once again been drawn. Advancing troops were on one side, the blacks—thousands of them now—mobbed on the other, protected by their flimsy iron shields.

Barrabas felt like a sleepwalker, unable to awaken from a terrible nightmare. He didn't know where he was going, and what he was leading his mercs into. He didn't even know whom to shoot at.

But from the looks of things, someone sure as hell deserved it. In the battle between white and black, they were on the bad side, though, and none of them could change the color of his skin.

Something urged him forward, farther into Soweto where there was no hiding in the no-man's-land between battle lines drawn by race.

Another volley of rifle shots announced the progress of the South African troops. Again the acrid stinging smell of tear gas floated by and mingled with the screams of fleeing protesters. Hundreds of them turned and ran up side streets from the intersections, pursued by troops swinging their heavy truncheons furiously.

Suddenly the alleyway in which the mercs had taken refuge was a melee of shouts and screams.

Hundreds of blacks, most of them young men and women and teenagers ran toward them.

"Get back!" Barrabas shouted over the noise. The mercs darted between a high wooden fence and an outbuilding in someone's backyard.

The riot troops started firing.

Bodies dropped suddenly to the gravel in front of them and just as quickly, security troops stormed past. Shots rang out from all directions. Most of the troops kept going, pursuing more demonstrators. Several stopped over the bodies of their victims, kicking and beating. Then an officer walked past, slowly and calmly firing his handgun into the heads of the fallen rioters.

Enough was enough.

This was butchery.

Barrabas raised his Uzi.

As the noise from the heavy march of boots and the wails of Soweto people swept across the township, Claude Hayes walked quickly in the shadows of side streets, circling in a wide arc around the riot to get to Samora's house.

His evasion was of no use. The riot came to him.

He turned a corner and ahead of him, a hundred feet down the street, demonstrators ran in their flight to safety. Not far behind, a line of troops marched solidly forward behind the protection of their plastic shields. The front line went down on their knees, like a curtain falling away from the soldiers behind them. They were the ones with guns.

They fired.

Two of the fleeing rioters fell in their tracks, bloody red flowers blooming across their backs.

The black American beat his club nervously against his thigh, trying to size up the situation. It was pretty hopeless. Unarmed civilians against soldiers with guns was not his definition of a fair fight.

The first line of troops was up again, moving relentlessly forward in their sweep. The demonstrators had regrouped down the street and the space between the opposing sides was thick with rock and glass missiles, the jeering shouts of the black Africans and the heavy even beat of marching feet.

Hayes was caught in the middle. He backed slowly into a laneway, looking behind him to find a way out. He slammed into the rusting hulk of an old car, tireless and set up on blocks against the back of a house. He turned fast enough to see a head duck behind the fender.

Hayes called to the hidden person in Swahili. There was no answer. Carefully, he circled the old car, gripping his club tightly in case he needed it.

He didn't.

The man playing hide-and-seek was badly wounded, almost unconscious and breathing heavily. A white man. He leaned against the car, clutching the side of his body. His shirt dripped red, and his face was contorted by pain. He opened his eyes and saw the big black man towering over him. Suddenly panic-stricken, he tried desperately to push himself back along the ground.

"Hey, it's okay," Hayes said in English, almost as if he was soothing a frightened animal. "It's okay."

The man stopped and stared at him with wide eyes. Hayes knelt down beside him.

It was Paul Krudd.

The young man stared up at Hayes without responding. The American reached down and felt the wound in Paul's chest.

"I worked at the mine. I saw you there today. I saw Peter give you the diamonds."

"You're an American," Paul said painfully. Claude's accent was unmistakable.

He nodded. "Are they looking for you?" The noise of the riot on the nearby streets continued.

"I think so," Paul replied. "The security police found out about me. Will you help?"

"Sure. You've got a fairly serious wound, though. In your back and out your chest. It missed your lungs, but you've lost a few ribs. Can you walk?"

"Not well. But I can try. If I can..."

"Lean on me. If I have to, I'll carry you."

Hayes helped the young American to his feet. Paul leaned heavily against him, his arm around Hayes's shoulder, while Hayes supported him with one hand under his arm.

"Where were you heading?" Claude asked him.

"I had instructions to a safehouse. A man named Samora. But I lost them when I..." Paul grimaced as another jolt of pain shot through his body.

Hayes reflected on the underground network that brought people to safety.

"Okay. I can take you there. We have to cross the police lines, though."

Paul nodded his head urgently. "I can do it."

The merc walked the young man out of the lane to the street. The troops had already gone past, sweeping the rioters farther into the township. The road was littered with broken glass, and several bodies lay limp and battered like forgotten garbage. Pariah dogs sniffed at them.

With Paul leaning on Hayes, the two men walked down the street toward the intersection at the bottom.

The sounds of rioting, shouts mixed with shotgun blasts, came from every side and grew louder.

The fighting returned so quickly that it came upon them before either man knew what to do. Mobs of people running, screaming and hurling missiles of stone and glass rushed out from the side streets into the intersection.

The troops surged forward, steadily behind them. More volleys of gunfire cut down protesters.

Paul was exhausted, his weight collapsing against Hayes. He'd lost blood—a lot of it. Hayes gripped tightly on the arm Paul had slung over his shoulder and picked the man up enough to run across the open street. He darted behind the line of the chanting crowd for protection from bullets and bottles. They crossed the street.

They had one more to cross.

One too many.

The line of riflemen parted, and columns of guards spilled through into the intersection. Their truncheons swung right and left like orchestra conductors cracking a symphony of heads.

The crowds of blacks turned and ran, panicked and fear ridden, falling over one another in their desperate hurry to get out of the way. Their comrades fell right and left as the security troops swung their clubs and reaped a bloody harvest of bodies collapsed on the pavement.

With the fury of their onslaught, the soldiers melted into the frenzied crowd like the blade of a hot knife through ice.

Hayes grabbed Paul Krudd tightly as rioters rushed past, bumping into them in their blind retreat. Hayes stumbled under the weight of the wounded white man. He tightened his face and grunted to squeeze more strength into his grip. He had twenty feet to go. He looked at the distance.

And started running.

Too late.

A trooper, big and ugly, confronted him, his blood-covered truncheon poised above Claude Hayes's head. He smashed it down.

15

The South African soldier looked up and saw Barrabas as the American merc fired his Uzi. The little submachine gun spurted its 9mm heavyweight hello into the officer's arm. He yelled and dropped his gun as the limb ripped in two lengthwise and spewed blood.

Two nearby soldiers turned to see their officer stagger under the load of pain. They raised their rifles and pointed to the shadows where the mercs stood.

Nanos and Bishop beat them to it. More Uzi greetings sparked in the dark. The soldiers' rifles flew behind them and they screamed in horror. Their hands and arms turned into chewed pulp dripping blood.

"Come on, let's go!" Barrabas ordered. The four mercs spun from their concealed place and ran down the alley toward the intersection, leaving the three soldiers to contemplate Barrabas's excruciating lesson.

The mercs ran hard and fast into the intersection.

All hell had broken loose.

The divisions between the white side and the black side were completely gone. Soweto was a total battle zone.

Rocks and bottles versus bullets and tear gas. Buildings along the intersection were in flames. Knots of demonstrators hurled their feeble missiles at the security troops and quickly fled, only to regroup fifty feet away. The security police formed a line of plastic shields and marched forward, suddenly finding that the rioters had cut around behind them. Cans of tear gas spun lazily along the street, spreading their fumes in all directions. Medics ran from the armored trucks lined up along the road that led out of Soweto, carrying choking, gasping troopers to safety. The black victims stayed where they fell.

Women and children flooded out of the buildings along the streets as the flames spread. Windows and doors from house to house were smashed by the heavy boots and truncheons of the troopers.

The bullets spared no one.

Barrabas watched the horror show with the glimmering firelight bathed across his sweat-soaked face.

"There's nothing we can do," he said to the others. "No black will let us near to help."

"Yeah, and fuck the whites," Bishop said.

In the battle of rocks against rifles, rifles win hands down. The troops had regrouped, forming a solid phalanx against one side of the square. They were pushing forward.

The Soweto rioters yielded ground, pegging their weapons back against the troops to slow their progress, then retreating up the street, past the entrance to the alley where the mercs watched.

"Colonel!" Nanos pointed with the barrel of his gun. "Over there!"

Barrabas saw it before Nanos finished speaking. A white man, drenched in blood and teetering on the brink of unconsciousness was being helped across the street by a big black guy. The black guy had his back turned to them. But the white guy was unmistakable. It was Paul Krudd.

Suddenly the line of troops parted, and a second wave bearing truncheons broke through. The SOBs ran into the melee in an attempt to get to Paul Krudd. No one appeared to notice their skin color in the general panic to escape the deadly South African soldiers. The soft popping sounds of another tear-gas volley signaled the onslaught. Canisters spewing plumes of abrasive smoke bounced along the road and fogged the air.

"We'll take care of these," Nanos cried, holding his breath and grabbing one. He hurled it back at the advancing line of troops. Bishop grabbed a second one and bounced it the same way. A South African soldier suddenly towered over him, his club ready to bash in the Canadian's head.

But Nanos was there. The truncheon came down on the barrel of the Greek's Uzi. Alex pulled it back and swung it into the trooper's belly. The man doubled over in agony and the big Greek smashed the Uzi across the back of his shoulders. He rolled on the ground, unconscious.

"I owe you one," Bishop said, looking at the Greek.

Nanos looked him square in the eyes. "Two," he said.

While Nanos and Bishop fended off their attackers, Barrabas and Lee Hatton ran for Paul Krudd. The black man helping Paul sagged under the wounded man's weight, his back turned to the mercs. He was trying to get the white man across the street. He wasn't going to make it.

A South African trooper towered over him, his bloody truncheon raised high to strike a blow.

Lee Hatton got there first.

There weren't many openings in the South African's body armor to make him vulnerable. Just a couple. She kneed up under his bulletproof vest and hit his groin. His eyes whitened in agony. Then her small fist hit him square in the throat. The truncheon fell to the ground. He had other things to worry about now. Like breathing.

Nile Barrabas grabbed the other half of Paul Krudd's sagging body and helped the black man hustle him across the street to the sidewalk. Then the two men looked each other in the face.

"Holy hell!" Barrabas broke into a big smile. "I don't believe it."

Claude Hayes followed with one of his own. "Welcome to the combat zone, Colonel! You on their side or our side?"

Barrabas didn't have to think about it. "Your side, Claude. And I brought our friends."

Lee Hatton took one look at Claude and threw her arms around his neck, planting a big kiss on his cheek.

"You're supposed to be dead," she yelled to get through the racket of the riot. She wiped her eyes, which stung from the tear gas.

"Nine lives," Hayes joked with a big happy smile at seeing the only friends he had. But across the intersection, another volley of bird shot struck the rioters. Someone was throwing Molotovs. Black and orange clouds burned on ponds of gasoline on the road and spread quickly across the gravel to an armored personnel carrier. Three soldiers climbed out madly as the flames licked their way up the sides.

Bishop and Nanos streaked across the intersection and ground to a halt beside their leader as hundreds of blacks ran past them down the street. The troops were advancing again, firing steady volleys of bird shot at the fleeing hordes. The litter of bodies in the streets of Soweto grew thicker.

No-nonsense Nanos took one fast look at Claude Hayes, and without registering any surprise, pointed his finger. "You alive?"

"Uh-huh. I'm alive."

Good enough for the Greek. "Then let's get the hell out of here!"

"Lead, Claude!" Barrabas ordered. He grabbed Paul Krudd's arms and pulled the young man over his shoulder.

Hayes took off, hugging the sides of the brick buildings along the street. Hatton and Nanos followed. Soon the mercs were lost in the general panic as hundreds of the angry demonstrators dived for cover inside buildings and down side streets.

Hayes led them into a narrow lane, through yards and between houses. The maze of Soweto streets soon overwhelmed their sense of direction. But the sounds of battle grew distant behind them. Soon Hayes had brought them to the little house with the curving horns of the impala crowning the door. They were barely in view when a beautiful young black woman burst from the house and ran to Paul.

"Quickly, into the house," Hayes told them.

Barrabas carried the unconscious man up the steps. A spidery little man wearing a thick wool blanket waited at the door with a wide-eyed boy of twelve or thirteen.

"I am Samora. Come quickly." He led Barrabas inside and pointed to the bed. "Put him there."

A moment later, the other mercenaries crowded into the little house. Lee Hatton immediately bent over the wounded man, carefully pulling his clothing open and assessing the seriousness of the injury.

"You cannot stay," Samora told Barrabas quickly. "The police will search here, too."

"How much time do we have?" Barrabas asked.

"Perhaps ten minutes." Already it seemed the sounds of the rioting and the storming of Soweto were coming closer.

"We have a Land Rover. Just inside Soweto, off Main Reef Road."

"And you have papers to pass through the soldiers' lines?"

Barrabas nodded.

"Hector!" Samora snapped his finger at the boy who listened silently, staring at the white faces around him. The African witch doctor spoke quickly in a Bantu dialect to the boy, and turned back to Barrabas.

"He will guide you another way to the vehicle. You must bring it here. Then Athustra—" he pointed to the young woman leaning over Paul "—will show you to a safe place."

"Alex! Geoff!" Barrabas summoned his two soldiers. "Go with the boy."

Hector looked up at Nanos and Bishop.

"You follow quickly," he said in English, running to the door. Nanos and Bishop flew after him.

Samora walked over to Lee Hatton, who was tending Paul Krudd's wound.

She shook her head hopelessly. "I have to sew him up. But I think he's lost too much blood. If we don't stop his bleeding, he won't survive."

"I assume you are a doctor," Samora said to her.

Lee nodded.

He turned to Athustra. "Bring water for washing. Hurry!" Then he rummaged in a nearby cupboard and brought out a black leather bag. "I was a doctor once, too. I have some things here." Lee looked in the bag. She found sterile sutures, needles, clamps and gauze.

"There is also this," Samora said. He held up a glass bottle containing an amber liquid. Lee stared at it, clearly mystified.

"When I was a doctor, I learned that European medicine did not have a monopoly on healing. My people call this a magical potion. In fact, it is merely a herbal liquid, prepared from the baobab tree." Samora poured some of the liquid into a cotton swab and began wiping the blood away from the wound. Almost miraculously, the bleeding stopped.

Athustra returned with a basin of steaming water and a sponge. Hatton set to work immediately, pulling the bloody clothing away and cleaning the skin. She glanced at the young woman who watched intently beside her. Her concern was obviously more than comradely. Love, and the fear of losing it, was written in her eyes.

As Lee and Samora went to work on the wounded Paul, Barrabas stared intently at Claude Hayes. In the sudden respite from the riots outside, they were, for the moment, speechless.

The black man smiled sheepishly. "Colonel, it's good to see you."

"Better to see you, Claude. You're supposed to be dead. We received intelligence information that you were among those killed on the Mozambique border in that raid two weeks ago."

"Two weeks ago." Hayes sighed wearily. "It seems like a lifetime." He explained the story of the diamonds. "The contact was Paul Krudd," he said, looking at the bed.

"That might explain why he was so hostile to us," Barrabas said. "He didn't trust anyone who looked like they were cooperating with the authorities."

"Why the hell are you here, Colonel?"

"Bishop Toto's consecration in Johannesburg is tomorrow. We were sent to inspect the security arrangements for it, as some kind of concession to the American government. There are rumors in intelligence circles that Toto is to be assassinated."

"Right now, all the African leaders are in prison except for the bishop," said Hayes. "He's the last hope. Not just for the blacks, either. It won't be long before this country erupts into a bloodbath."

"And the whites are pushed into the sea from the beaches of Cape Town?"

"Twenty-two million Africans are enslaved for cheap labor by seven million whites who own everything. And they're not doing much to change that."

"I know," Barrabas told him. "And since we arrived here two days ago, we've been deliberately stonewalled by the people we're supposed to work with. We've accomplished nothing."

"You found us!" Hayes flashed a big toothy smile. "And now you're going to get us out of here."

"Colonel Barrabas," Samora called from the bed. "Paul is talking."

Barrabas strode to the bed where Lee Hatton deftly drew stitches through the tattered skin on Paul's chest wound.

"We must hurry," Samora whispered anxiously. The sounds of smashing doors, breaking glass and troops running through Soweto streets were growing louder. The South African army continued their house-to-house search for Paul Krudd.

"Only a few more," Lee said.

"I have given him a narcotic," Samora explained. "He does not feel pain now."

Paul opened his eyes. He looked at the people who were gathered around him as if he stood a great distance away. His eyes stopped on the features of Nile Barrabas.

Samora kneeled at the bed near his head and spoke softly to the young man. "These are our friends. They will take you from here soon. You must tell them what you told me."

Paul's eyes flicked away from Barrabas's face and he stared at the ceiling.

"Finished," Lee announced. She snipped the last suture and began dressing the bloodless wound with gauze.

Paul looked at Barrabas again and spoke. His voice quavered and lacked strength.

"Bishop Toto, the one who will be consecrated tomorrow, is an impostor." Paul stopped and watched the American colonel. Barrabas waited without reacting. Paul looked at Samora. The thin little man squeezed some water against the wounded man's lips from a clean cotton cloth.

"Go on," Samora urged. "You must tell them everything."

"They've made a substitution. The real bishop is a prisoner somewhere. Tomorrow in Johannesburg they will provoke a riot. The impostor will say things that will make the crowd riot. He will be killed by his own people."

"And where is Toto?" Barrabas asked.

Paul shook his head slightly. "Don't know. But still alive. A prisoner somewhere. They'll kill him later."

"Who's behind this?" Barrabas kneeled lower to hear the young man speak.

Paul's eyes floated away dreamily, as if he had lost interest.

"Who's behind this?" Barrabas grabbed Paul's chin and jerked the young man's eyes open.

"Major Snider. Others. Van den Boos, Miller, Bloemvaal…" His voice trailed as he slipped away into unconsciousness again.

"Paul!" Barrabas spoke firmly, leaning over Paul's face. "Who else?"

The young man came back from his narcotic stupor again. He gazed into Barrabas's eyes.

"And my father," he said simply. His eyes closed and his head rolled sideways. Consciousness left him.

"Finished," Hatton said as she wound gauze bandages around the man's chest and clipped them together.

The door banged open and Nanos walked in.

"Hey, Colonel! Catch!" He hurled two grenades at Barrabas. Both hands went out to grab them. Barrabas examined them and threw one back to the Greek.

"Where the hell did you find these?"

"A wounded soldier lying behind the police lines had them clipped to his belt. The riot troops here come prepared for unarmed civilians. Definitely prepared."

Barrabas slipped the grenade into the pocket on the side of his pants for later use.

Geoff Bishop stood at the door of the little house. "The soldiers are a block away and coming fast," he announced.

"Quickly," Samora urged them. He threw a blanket over Paul.

Claude Hayes lifted the man from the bed and carried him outside.

"Are you coming?" Barrabas asked Samora.

The old man shook his head. "No, I will be safe here. Go. Hurry. The spirit of Kwati Umba, the Eternal Warrior, is with you. You will be safe, too." He smiled a little. "He will help you save our country."

16

Hayes laid Paul Krudd carefully on the floor in the back of the Land Rover. Athustra climbed in and lay beside him. He covered them both with the blanket.

Bishop drove, with Barrabas riding shotgun, Hatton and Nanos in the back seat and Hayes wedged down in the space remaining at their feet. By this time, he knew the way blind, calling the directions to Bishop by watching the tops of the houses from his vantage point below the window.

The soldiers had reached the end of the street. Groups of them went from house to house in relays, with other soldiers standing guard or marching away the occasional black prisoner. The battle continued, but somewhere else. Thousands of voices raised in protest could still be heard in the distance. Soldiers eyed the Land Rover curiously as it rolled by, but few paid much attention to the Americans.

As they drove through the intersection that had been a combat zone only a few minutes earlier, they saw a gravel truck with its tailgate down, receiving a grisly load. Soldiers piled bodies into it like cordwood.

At the edge of Soweto, the highway was a sea of police and security cars, army trucks and field-communications vans. Bishop braked in front of a party of armed men who lined the road. A beef-faced sergeant sauntered to the window. Barrabas leaned out and flashed his papers.

"Oh," the sergeant said suspiciously. "The Americans." His lips tightened, and he looked at them distastefully. He stood back and waved them through.

But Barrabas wasn't finished. He opened his door and stuck his head up over the roof as the sergeant walked away. "Hey, bud!"

The sergeant didn't like that. But Barrabas was a VIP.

"Yeah, mack?"

"Where's Snider? Major Snider."

The sergeant shook his head. "Headquarters, in Johannesburg. He'll be there all night." The South African soldier jerked his head at a party of prisoners being marched away at rifle point, hands manacled behind their backs, to a waiting paddy wagon. "We rounded up a bit of work for him," he said ominously, but with obvious pleasure.

Barrabas got back in, and Bishop eased the Land Rover forward through the military traffic.

"Colonel, did you check out what's going on over here?" Bishop asked him, motioning out the window on his side of the vehicle.

Helicopters hovered and landed on an improvised landing zone in a field. Portable lights surrounded the area, and soldiers flagged the choppers down. The brass was arriving for a little look-see.

"Those are old Kiowas, stretch 206-Ls," said Bishop, a man who knew his flying machines. "We sure could use one of them," he hinted.

"Damn right," Barrabas said. "Alex, Lee," he called into the back seat. "You want to help Geoff commandeer that copter we were supposed to pick up earlier today?"

"I'd love to." Nanos was panting for action.

"What about me, Colonel?" The question came from Claude Hayes, who was still crouched down out of sight on the floor of the Land Rover.

"I've got something else in mind for you, Claude." Barrabas turned back to Bishop. "Pull over by the brown Rolls-Royce up there." He pointed to Krudd's elegant car, sitting alone at the far end of the long line of vehicles parked on the shoulder of the road that led out of Soweto. The traffic here was reduced to the occasional paddy wagon that drove out of the township with its load of prisoners.

The other mercs recognized Krudd's car immediately.

"What are you going to do, Colonel?" Bishop asked.

"See if Mr. Krudd knows how to make healthy decisions. When should I meet you on the landing zone?"

"Well," Bishop started, "if we're not back in fifteen..."

"Forget us and get the hell out," Nanos muttered, checking his pockets for mag supplies. He and Lee crammed a few more of the 9mm Uzi mags into their pockets. Bishop pulled the Land Rover over behind the Rolls and the mercs jumped out.

Lee ran into the dark grass off the road, with Nanos and Bishop right behind her. They circled in a wide arc that led them away from the road and behind the landing zone. The land rose slightly on one side, allowing them to lie on their stomachs on the crest of the incline and watch the action from a dozen yards away.

Three helicopters were parked to one side. One had just taken off and another one was coming in. A panel truck with the side open was filled with communications equipment, and a guy wearing earphones was plugged in to it.

"Okay, there're two ways of doing this," said Alex. "The first is to go in there, take a chopper and if anyone tries to stop us, we blow them away."

"That's a good idea, Alex," Geoff Bishop said, unconvinced. "What's the second way?"

"Go in there, take a chopper and blow away anyone who tries to stop us."

The Greek was a simple man, easily satisfied.

"Alex, you're..."

"I'm what, Bishop?"

"Hey, easy..."

"Can it, you guys." It was Lee's turn to calm them down. "Look who's coming." She pointed to a couple of helicopter pilots approaching the communications van, zipping up their leather jackets. They looked as though they were going somewhere.

"There's a way of doing this without them even knowing about it. You guys move around to where those three helicopters are parked. I'll sneak up beside the communications van and find out which one's going out first. After that..."

"Got it!" It was so obvious that Bishop thought it was brilliant.

"How'll you signal us which copter to get into?" Nanos asked.

"I could flick a cigarette lighter. With all these flashing lights around, no one will notice that."

"I don't have one. I don't smoke," Nanos pointed out.

"Neither do I," Bishop added.

"Geez, I wish you guys would take up some bad habits besides bitching at each other. Forget it. I'll make sure I'm there before the pilots are. Don't forget to do this, guys." She dug her hands into the soil and smeared dark earth over her face.

"Good idea," Nanos said, and the two mercs followed Hatton's lead.

"Yeah. Just think. We wouldn't have to do this if our skin was the right color," she commented ironically.

Then she was off, crawling on her belly through the high grass, propelling herself forward with her elbows and knees.

Nanos and Bishop retreated behind the hillock to circle around and come up behind the parked helicopters.

As Lee got closer she saw the two pilots chatting and drinking coffee from paper cups. The communications operator was talking impatiently into his microphone, trying to get someone at the other end to answer. From time to time he turned to the pilots to roll his eyes. The pilots laughed understandingly.

Hatton reached the van. Very slowly, and keeping her weight off the ground to avoid noise, she moved underneath it.

"Number two, boys," the radio operator said. "And make it snappy. I got a bird on its way in, and I want you guys out of here right now."

Lee was just in time for the orders to come through.

But too late to get the word back to Nanos and Bishop.

THE GREEK AND THE CANADIAN PILOT approached the parked helicopters just as they saw the pilots running in their direction.

"What'll we use to..." Nanos started to ask.

Bishop anticipated him by unclipping the canvas strap on his Uzi. Alex understood.

"They're going for the second one," Bishop said, seeing one of the pilots point.

"Hatton!" Nanos reminded him.

"She'll get here."

The two men darted out of the grass and ran to the edge of the landing zone. The back door to the chopper was open. Bishop went first. He climbed in and stayed down behind the front seat. A moment later, Alex took his place beside him. When the two pilots reached the Kiowa, they went for opposite doors, strapping themselves into the pilot's and copilot's seats. The pilot turned on the panel lights and started the engine. They didn't bother to look over their shoulders.

Big mistake.

The thin canvas straps fitted neatly over their heads and around their necks with a quick flick. Nanos and Bishop tightened in unison.

Both pilots grabbed at their throats, trying to get a fingerhold on the tight bands cutting into their necks. Their bodies heaved. All instincts went on alert as they fought to live. Their tongues stretched obscenely from their mouths.

Bishop squeezed tighter as his victim struggled and squirmed. He prayed silently for it to be fast for the poor guy.

It seemed to take forever.

Finally the pilot's movements slowed. Life emptied from his body. The man slumped slowly sideways. Nanos's victim lasted only a few seconds longer.

Cooperating silently and swiftly, the Greek helped Bishop drag the dead man from the pilot's seat, pulling him into the back.

Bishop immediately stripped the man's jacket off.

"Hey, there's a guy with a flashlight waving his arms at us and yelling."

"It's the flagman—he wants us to take off," Bishop said quickly, pulling the dead man's jacket on.

"Quick! He's coming this way!"

"Straighten up the other body." Bishop saw a hat dangling from the cyclic handle. He put it on.

Nanos looked at the recently garroted body of the copilot. It was going to be messy no matter how he did it. He reached around the neck and poked the man's tongue back in his mouth. The eyes were still open.

Bishop climbed into the pilot's seat.

"What's the holdup?" and impatient voice barked outside. The flagman was four yards away from the chopper window.

Bishop upped the revs and turned on the outside lights. The blades began to turn faster. He rolled down the window.

"No problem. My copilot just had a leak."

"Well get that thing the hell out of here and have a leak some other—"

The rotors drowned out the voice of the irate flagman as Bishop lifted the chopper into a low hover.

"Hatton!" Nanos whispered vehemently from the back.

"We'll get her." Bishop brought the chopper up higher and turned it in the direction of the lights of Johannesburg.

Two more helicopters were landing just as they lifted off, providing a distraction for the flagman and anyone else who might have been watching. Bishop took the helicopter out over the field, lifting gradually.

"You notice what's sticking out of the side of this chopper?" Bishop shouted back to Nanos.

Nanos looked. The Kiowa was side-armed.

"It's an XM-27 gun kit," Bishop finished. "Controls are up here in the copilot's panel."

"Great! It makes us one big flying machine gun. Without Hatton!" he reminded Bishop.

"Watch for her!"

The Greek was already searching out the side window. Bishop shut off the lights, casting them into the darkness of night. He slowed and dropped down, circling back in the direction of the landing zone. He kept his eyes on the zone, trying to estimate where the mercenary would be if she was circling around to the parked helicopters.

LEE HATTON SAW THE HELICOPTER take off before she was halfway around the landing zone. She cursed, throwing her Uzi back over her shoulder and running for the road. She kept her eye on the Kiowa as it skimmed higher across the field, not knowing if Nanos and Bishop were aboard. Suddenly the helicopter disappeared in the night sky. Then she knew. The chopper was theirs.

She didn't hear it coming back until it was almost overhead because of the racket from other incoming helicopters on the landing zone.

She felt the air moving above her as she ran, and the noise of a chopper suddenly rolled over her. When she looked up, she saw the great dark silhouette descending like a bird of prey. She stopped and waved at it, hoping they could see her. But dark clothes and camouflaged skin works both ways. She needed something white to wave at them. There was only one thing she could think of.

She quickly ripped open her shirt, pulling it down off her arms, and unfastened her bra. She waved it at the helicopter. It turned, its dark eye spotting her. She tossed the bra aside and ran for it.

The machine was skimming shoulder height over the earth as she panted behind it, her feet barely touching the ground. She became acutely conscious of the blind pain from a stitch in her side. The back door opened. She was breathing raggedly, pushing herself to go faster. A hand stretched out. Nanos. She knew enough about helicopters to know that Bishop was having problems keeping the speed down in that kind of holding position. Sure enough, just when it seemed her own speed was fast enough to catch up, the helicopter pulled ahead slightly.

She could hear Alex yelling urgently over the heavy sounds of the rotor. His arm waved frantically at the door. She clenched her teeth and ran faster. Nanos stretched from the door, gripping a hold bar to keep himself from tumbling out. Lee reached for his hand; she was short by a foot. The helicopter pulled ahead, and Lee ran faster.

Alex stretched. Their fingers brushed, then overlapped. Hands groped for hands, catching. Nanos wound his steel grip around Lee's wrist and pulled.

Lee left the ground as the helicopter floated upward, and Nanos pulled her up to the door. She grabbed for the rim of the floor and caught it. Nanos pulled again and she brought her legs up, kicking them in the open door. She flew into the fuselage on her stomach with her arm still hanging out the rear doorplate.

The Greek pushed her in and pulled the door shut.

"You okay?" Bishop shouted from the pilot's seat. All Lee could do was swallow and nod as she caught her breath. Her lungs ached.

"Yeah, she's all right," Alex called up front. He was almost as out of breath as she was. Lee was still barechested, an Amazon with her shirt pulled down and the Uzi strap crossing between the cleavage.

Both realized it as they caught their breath. They laughed, and Lee pulled her shirt back up.

"So that's what I saw waving down here," Alex said.

"I didn't think you'd miss a brassiere, Alex," Lee said with a laugh, taking the Uzi off to button up. "Let's get rid of that," she said pointing to the body of the pilot slumped in the front seat, "and see how the colonel's making out.

IN THE LAND ROVER, Barrabas stripped off his jacket and unfastened the straps on his shoulder holster. He handed Claude Hayes the Browning Hi-Power and fished an extra 13-round mag of 9mm parabellum from his pocket.

"That should keep me going for a minute," Hayes remarked, strapping the holster on.

"At least until we get you an automatic rifle," said Barrabas.

"I had an AK-47 when I came into South Africa," Hayes commented, pulling the straps tight. "Traded it for some money and food. You can't eat bullets."

"Wait here with Paul and the woman," Barrabas instructed him. "I'm going to make Krudd chew on this." He waved his Uzi. "If he doesn't come up with some answers, he's going to have serious indigestion."

He left the Land Rover and walked to the Rolls. Krudd was at the wheel. Barrabas tapped on the window, startling him. When Krudd looked out and saw the white-haired American colonel, he reached to the door panel to press the automatic door-locking switch. Barrabas knocked on the glass again. With the barrel of his gun.

The window slid down silently, and Krudd stared at the gun pointed right between his eyes.

"Shove over," Barrabas ordered. He pressed the snub-nosed Uzi hard into the man's soft chest, pulled the door release and pushed into the car. Krudd retreated to the passenger side. He opened his mouth to protest, and Barrabas shoved the barrel of the Uzi in.

"Chew on that, Krudd. And while you're thinking about what a few rounds will do to your brain, you can tell me where the real Bishop Toto is hidden."

Krudd began to shake. Saliva welled up in his open mouth and dripped down the barrel of the Uzi.

"I uuuuh ooo!" he said, with his tongue wrapped around steel oblivion.

"What do you mean you don't know, Krudd? Watch my finger on the trigger. And think about those bullets boring their way through your head and splattering your cortex on the window behind you."

Barrabas jabbed the Uzi forward, pushing Krudd's mouth farther open and head back. The man was shaking with fear, his teeth chattering on the metal barrel.

"I uuu ooo," Krudd screeched.

Barrabas eased back on the trigger. The man was trembling uncontrollably.

"Who does know?"

"Sniyer," he said, his tongue still bouncing off the barrel of the submachine gun.

"Where's Snider now?" To reward him, Barrabas withdrew the Uzi halfway from his mouth.

"Johannesburg."

"Well, maybe you better tell me how I can get in touch with him, because if I don't I might get angry enough to blow off your head."

Barrabas pulled the Uzi from the man's mouth and brushed it slowly along Krudd's lips. He kept it there. Krudd's shaking subsided. But his eyes stayed glued to the threatening snub nose of the Uzi.

"We're meeting at the house," he gulped. "At 6:00 A.M. To prepare for the consecration. He'll be there."

"Very good, Krudd."

"What will you do...with me?"

"That depends on how useful you are. First of all, I'm going to back out of the car. I want you to come forward very slowly. Then we'll go over to the Land Rover. Understand?"

Krudd nodded his head eagerly. He understood, and with an Uzi stuck in his face, he was anxious to co-operate. Barrabas pulled the keys from the ignition just in case. He slid back on the seat and pushed the door open. As he stood outside on the road he grabbed the lapels of Krudd's jacket and pulled the man out after him. Then he marched him over to the Land Rover.

"Lean against the roof!"

Krudd hesitated. He wasn't used to following orders. Barrabas grabbed him with one powerful hand and spun him around, pushing him against the side of the four-wheel and throwing his hands up over the roof. Then he stuck the barrel of his Uzi in Krudd's back, carefully positioning the snout over his spinal cord.

"Hayes," he called inside the car. The black warrior slid out of the passenger seat.

"What time is it?" Barrabas asked.

"Midnight."

"Krudd says only Snider knows where the real Bishop Toto is, and Snider isn't available until he goes to the Krudd estate at six this morning."

"You believe him, Colonel?"

Barrabas pondered a couple of seconds. "I don't know, Claude. But other than killing him, all we can do is give him the benefit of the doubt."

"That gives us six hours. I don't know if I want to hang around this place." Across the field, Soweto burned and the highway behind them still swarmed with police and troops.

"I was thinking," Barrabas said to Hayes. "You want to get that diamond?"

Hayes nodded.

"Well, it looks like we've got a few hours to kill, and we've got ourselves a ticket into the mine." He jabbed the Uzi into Krudd's back to make him squirm.

"Sounds good to me, Colonel. What about Paul and the girl?"

Krudd started when he heard his son's name.

"Yeah, that's right, Krudd. Your son Paul is safe. Right inside the Land Rover," Barrabas told him.

"Claude, can you take over here? I'll go inside and talk to them."

Hayes pulled the Browning from his holster. He grabbed the back of Krudd's head and pushed his face into the metal frame of the Land Rover.

"Kiss it, baby!" He shoved the barrel of the Browning against the nape of Krudd's neck. "Take your time, Colonel."

Barrabas got into the back of the Land Rover and looked over the seat at Paul and Athustra. The woman was sitting up. She was frightened but calm. Paul lay on the floor. His eyes were open and bright. He was conscious.

"How are you two doing?" Barrabas asked.

"We're fine, Colonel." It was Paul who answered. The lovely black woman rested her hand on his chest and looked at him. Paul's voice was firm. He was going to live.

"Where is this safe place Samora mentioned?" Barrabas asked the woman.

"Lesotho," she said. Lesotho was a tiny, independent country south of Johannesburg, completely surrounded by South Africa. It was like an island of African freedom in the middle of the white-ruled country. "If we go across the border there, we can fly anywhere to safety."

"Can you drive?" Barrabas asked. "If you take the Rolls?"

The young woman nodded. "It will take about two and a half hours to reach the border."

"What about roadblocks?"

"I know roads that lead through the country. And in that car we will not be stopped."

Barrabas nodded. It was all going to work out. "Good. I want you to take Paul to Lesotho. We have some other business to take care of. Paul, do you have anything to say to your father?"

Paul looked for a moment at the white-haired merc before answering. His eyes fell. "No."

Barrabas turned to go outside.

"Wait!" Paul cried.

Barrabas closed the door again and leaned over to look at the young man as he spoke.

"I wanted to apologize, Colonel."

"For what?"

"For...not trusting you."

"You didn't know."

"Yes, but I should have. I never really thought about anything much until I came back to this country, you know. But when I saw it, well... My mother took me away from here when I was a kid because she wanted me to grow up an American like her. She used to say that an American knows right from wrong and a South African doesn't. And that when an American sees wrong, he does something about it. I couldn't bear what I saw here."

"So you did something."

"I tried."

"Well, from what Claude told me, you succeeded, too. It took a lot of courage."

"Athustra helped." Paul smiled at the beautiful young African woman. "It's illegal for us to be in love here. A white man and a black woman. Or even to make love."

"Two good reasons to get you both out of here." Barrabas grinned. They heard the sound of a helicopter growing louder over the distant din of the troop activity around Soweto.

"You can travel a bit?" he asked Paul. The wounded man nodded.

Barrabas opened the doors of the Land Rover and helped him sit up. The helicopter was pulling into a hover twenty feet off the road.

"Get Krudd in the copter," Barrabas ordered Hayes. Lee Hatton and Nanos ran through the windstream under the rotors.

Hayes and Hatton grabbed Krudd and took him to the chopper while Nanos helped Barrabas carry Paul to the front seat of the Rolls. Athustra got in behind the wheel and started the engine.

Barrabas flashed a quick wave and took off after Nanos. He had barely scrambled in the rear door when Bishop lifted the chopper up.

"Where to, Colonel?" Bishop yelled over the engine noise.

"East!" said Barrabas, sinking into a welcome seat. Wilhelm Krudd sat frozen next to him, his face pale, and his eyes darting furtively from the gun that Nanos held to the gun that Lee Hatton held. Both were pointed at him.

Barrabas aimed his in the same general direction and riveted his eyes on the corrupt plotter. Krudd shrunk visibly from the gaze.

"To the Krudd Diamond Mines. The owner will show us the way."

But Wilhelm Krudd did not look anxious to comply.

17

The private security force at the Krudd Diamond Mine saw the helicopter with security service markings as it flew over the electrified fence and descended to the ground.

The private guards who rushed for the arriving aircraft snapped to attention when Wilhelm Krudd appeared at the door and stepped out. The tall white-haired American, a woman and a black man were with him. Nanos and Bishop had switched uniforms with the dead pilots before their bodies were discarded. The charade was complete.

The commander of the guards strode forward to speak to Wilhelm Krudd. He eyed the industrialist's companions with a degree of suspicion. They were not the bodyguards that usually accompanied the mine owner.

"It's all right, Captain Jenkins," Krudd told the man. "These people work for me. Something's come up and I want to go down into the mine."

"Very well, sir." The private commander hesitated slightly as his eyes flicked over Barrabas and company. Krudd stayed cool. The officer stood to one side.

Krudd led the mercs across the yard and past the administrative buildings to the lift.

"Shall we dress, gentlemen? It's illegal to enter the mine without hard hats, overalls and the proper footwear."

Barrabas looked at Hayes.

"We need flashlights, or the helmets."

"Just helmets, Krudd. It's all we have time for."

He took them into the warehouse where locker rooms and showers indicated a change area. The building was well lit, and attendants mopped the floor, waiting for the night shift to return in a few hours from the depths beneath the earth's surface. Krudd requisitioned four helmets from an equipment employee with the snap of his fingers. The mercs descended on the booth where the lift operator was hunched over an instrument panel.

"Lee, stay here." Barrabas gave his order out of earshot of the lift operator. "Make sure that guy in there doesn't bring the lift back up before we're on it."

The woman mercenary nodded. She took up a position in the doorway of the booth where she could keep a careful eye on the man at the control panel.

Krudd led Barrabas and Hayes to the lift, and the three men rode the big cage on its slow descent to the thousand-foot level.

"I doubt you'll get away with this," Krudd said stiffly on the way down.

"Why not? We seem to be doing pretty good so far."

"Someone will suspect something." Krudd squirmed and adjusted his jacket lapels around the open collar of his shirt. "Our country is prepared for people like you."

Barrabas pressed the snub nose of his Uzi under Krudd's chin, pushing his head up. "Just remember this, Wilhelm. And make sure nothing goes wrong."

Krudd gulped.

The lift slowed to a stop in the big whitewashed cavern. It was deserted, but the sounds of miners digging the rock, the bins clattering on their steel rails and the shouts of the foremen could be heard echoing through the tunnels that led through the ancient volcanic pipes.

Hayes stopped outside for a minute to get his bearings.

"You remember the way?" Barrabas asked. He hoped it was a joke.

"I hope so, Colonel." And Hayes led off, shaking his head.

He started walking down the tunnel with Krudd behind him, and Barrabas last. A few minutes later, Hayes recognized the turnoff by the wooden barrier across the entrance and the broken machinery that blocked it. The darkness beyond was impenetrable.

They snapped their helmet lights on.

Just as they were about to turn, Hayes put out his hand to stop them. A party of miners was coming down the tunnel ahead of them, laughing and chatting, probably on their way to a coffee break.

As they came closer, Hayes recognized the big man in the centre of the group. Nkono.

"Oh, shit," he muttered under his breath.

The miners stopped talking when they caught sight of the two white men with Hayes. Nkono recognized the black American, and the miners slowed their pace behind Nkono. The big Xhosa boss glared at Hayes, his eyes filled with hatred. But they kept going.

Hayes breathed a sigh of relief.

"Who the hell was that?" Barrabas asked.

"It's a story. I'll tell you later." Hayes climbed over the wooden barrier and started through the tunnel.

The light from his helmet bobbed through the blackness. A few minutes later, they came to the end. Hayes kneeled on the rocky floor and began brushing at the stones and grit along the side of the wall. Soon he found the spot where the soil was loose. He pulled out the larger rocks.

"There it is," he said, wiping the dirt off the glassy side of the huge stone.

"That's a diamond?" Barrabas asked.

"When they're raw, they're not much to look at," Hayes said. He dug his hand into the wall and pulled more dirt and rocks aside. "But look at the size of it."

"Incredible," Krudd whispered in awe, forgetting for the moment his captivity.

Hayes continued to dig at the wall until the side of the giant crystal was clear. He inserted his fingers around the edge of it to get a grip. It didn't budge. He worked at it a few more minutes. Still it didn't move.

"Colonel, it's not going anywhere. We need some tools to smash the rock away and get it out."

"Can you get some?"

"Yeah."

"I'll wait here with Krudd."

Hayes disappeared into the blackness that separated them from the main shaft, retracing his steps until light shone around the broken machinery and he crossed over the wooden barrier again.

He had barely set his foot down on the other side when six big African miners stepped in front of him. The biggest man was in the center. Nkono. This time they all had clubs.

"Now, man, we teach you a lesson," Nkono said threateningly, shaking his club and taking a step forward.

Hayes quickly summed up his choices. Fight, flight or fast talking.

He chose the last one.

"Nkono. You must believe who I am. I come from...from the north of Africa. I am a fighter for the liberation of Azania. I need help. Not a battle with you, who are African like me."

Nkono didn't look convinced. He stepped forward. His five friends did the same.

Hayes became acutely aware of the cold steel Browning pressed against his skin under his shirt. It would make a lot of noise in the underground tunnels. But he'd use it if he had to.

Nkono stopped and grabbed a club from the miner beside him. He threw it at Hayes. The American caught it. "Fight me!" Nkono challenged. "And we will see once again who is stronger."

Hayes looked at the club and threw it contemptuously on the ground.

"I will not fight. We are brothers. I come to you as a brother for help. For the *chimurenga*."

The mention of the word that meant "freedom struggle" sent a ripple through the miners. They looked at one another and at their leader. Nkono hushed them quickly. The menacing look on his face remained. His hand visibly gripped tighter on his club. He took a second step toward Hayes.

Claude stood his ground.

"I come here to help with your struggle. Instead you want to fight me and not those who enslave you. Look!" he cried, grabbing his collar and with a mighty pull tearing his shirt. It ripped down off his shoulder and revealed the strange tattoo of the panther.

A chorus of amazement broke from the mouths of the Bantu workers.

When Claude Hayes led the freedom fighters in the Mozambique wars, he gave his men the sign of the panther as a talisman to protect them in battle. Maybe it was just Hayes's prowess as a warrior that allowed him to succeed in ambush and battle where ordinary soldiers failed to win. The tattoo of the panther became a sign of luck, of invincibility. The legend of Kwati Umba, the Eternal Warrior, had been born from it. And the power of the legend had swept across Africa to wherever men and women fought for their freedom.

Nkono stared at the vivid tattoo, drawn with powdered charcoal under the skin of Hayes's shoulder. He looked at Hayes and back at the tattoo. The expression on his face didn't change. Nkono's men waited silently, fearful of their leader's choice.

Suddenly, Nkono bent and picked up the knobbed club Hayes had thrown down. He handed it to Hayes. As a brother.

"For Kwati Umba," he said.

BARRABAS AND KRUDD WAITED SILENTLY for Hayes, with only the light from Barrabas's helmet breaking the thick darkness. They heard footsteps coming back up the tunnel. More than one man's. Several.

Barrabas threw Krudd behind him, crushing him against the wall and standing in front with his Uzi pointing down the tunnel. Half a dozen helmet lights bobbed in the darkness.

He heard Hayes's voice.

"It's all right, Colonel. I've brought some friends to help dig it out."

Nkono and his men went to work, bashing the rock wall with heavy steel rods and scooping away the debris. Quickly the giant diamond was carved out of the wall. It seemed to grow in size as it was revealed.

Nkono knelt on the floor and examined their progress. "An hour more if you want all of it," he said. "But we can break it off now. That will leave a little bit behind. Like this." He held his hands in the size of a grapefruit.

Hayes looked at Barrabas. "Break it," the white-haired mercenary said.

Hayes nodded at Nkono.

"No!" Krudd shouted.

They turned to look at him.

Krudd shrank from his own outburst. "If you try to break it, you might shatter the whole diamond," he explained. "Like a car window. It'll crumble to pieces."

"That's right," Barrabas confirmed. "It has to do with the stress lines. But to get the end out of the rock, we'll have to dig out a few feet all around it. That'll take time."

"Let's break it," Hayes said. He nodded at Nkono.

The miners gathered at the hole in the rock wall where the giant diamond sat like a football set in concrete. They inserted their steel pries behind the stone. Nkono gave them the signal.

Together they bashed the base of the stone and levered in, their muscles straining against solid rock. The giant diamond lurched forward with a sudden crack, and rolled out of the hole in one piece, coming to a stop at Hayes's feet.

The miners broke into smiles. Hayes and Nkono looked at each other, the menace between them replaced by respect.

One of the miners took off his shirt, wrapped the diamond and handed it to Hayes. It weighed almost twenty pounds.

Nkono raised his hand and Claude clasped it, thumbs locked in the handshake of comradeship. He turned to Barrabas and the silent, simpering Krudd.

"Colonel, let's go."

LEE HATTON WAS WAITING FOR THEM in the control booth at the surface when she saw Hayes carrying the diamond like a baby wrapped in swaddling clothes.

"That diamond is worth millions," Krudd muttered, as they hustled him along. "Millions!"

"It'll be worth even more to the underground here when it's put on display in Maputo as a symbol of their struggle," said Hayes.

"You'll never get away with it," Krudd threatened.

Barrabas eyed the industrialist. There was a new light in the man's eyes since they had located the diamond. As they retraced their steps to the helicopter, the man's eyes were searching right and left for an avenue of escape.

"Don't try it," Barrabas warned.

"Try what?"

"To make a run for it. If you gamble on us not shooting you with all your security people around, you're wrong." The colonel fervently hoped that Krudd wouldn't call his bluff.

Lee joined them as they walked quickly across the yard and into the change rooms where they took off their helmets.

Krudd bolted, running for the door to the yard.

"Get the diamond into the chopper," Barrabas ordered the other mercs. He took off after the escaping man.

Krudd crossed the yard with surprising speed, going for a pair of open double doors that led into another part of the mine. He had one major advantage over Barrabas. He knew where he was going.

Barrabas slid to a halt at the doorway to a huge, two-story plant housing machinery that processed the diamond-bearing rock. At one end of the long warehouse, conveyer belts carried the rock from outside a distance of several hundred feet to a ten-foot drop where the rock fell into giant crushers. Three-sided steel rollers pulverized it into gravel before it traveled on to strainers that removed the diamonds. The plant was empty at night, eerily lit by the outside spotlights shining against the opaque factory windows.

Krudd scrambled across the cement floor, sliding on his polished shoes to avoid bulky machinery. He made his way to some doors on the far side of the building.

Barrabas kept going.

Suddenly Krudd disappeared.

Barrabas stopped and listened carefully. The man could have hidden behind or under any one of a number of machines. His eyes adjusted to the shadows. He circled slowly along the length of the conveyer belt until he came to the control panel. He stood up on the desk and peered out over the floor, trying to catch a glimpse of movement.

Twenty feet away, Krudd made a break for it. He ran across an open space until he was confronted by the conveyer that cut the floor of the plant in two. He couldn't go under it because of machinery. He tried to scramble over, huffing and puffing to pull his weight across.

Barrabas looked down at the controls at his feet. The big green On button was clearly marked. He stomped on it with the toe of his boot just as Krudd stood up on the conveyer belt and started running to the end where the doorway marked his escape route. The hum of machinery and gears snapping into place presaged the movement of the conveyer, and with a grind and a jerk it started moving.

Caught by surprise, Krudd lost his balance and slammed down on his ass. He shrieked with pain and surprise. The belt rolled him forward toward the fall to the crushers.

He flipped over to push himself off, but overcome by paralyzing terror, he couldn't move. His scream froze in his throat. Finally one word came out. A little word, tiny and pitiful in his throat.

"Help!" he bleated.

The drop to the crushers was ten feet away. The conveyer moved inexorably on.

Barrabas looked down at the panel. The Stop button was as clearly marked as the On button. But that wasn't what he had in mind.

Right next to the drop at the end of the conveyer belt was a narrow metal staircase that led to a platform where workers could watch the crushers.

Barrabas jumped to the floor. He scaled the ladder and reached the top just as Krudd got to the end of the belt. The industrialist reached for Barrabas, his face pitiful with total fear. Barrabas dropped his Uzi to the metal floor and reached over the rail. He caught Krudd by the collar of his shirt, just as the conveyer belt came to its decisive end. Krudd's feet rolled over the edge into empty space. Ten feet below his dangling legs, the giant studded rollers gnashed like hungry teeth.

"Help me! Help me, please! Help me!" he whimpered and begged, grabbing for Barrabas's arm.

The colonel's fist strained to hold Krudd's weight. His veins bulged down the length of his arm, and his skin grew red with the infusion of blood.

"Don't touch my arm, Krudd!" Barrabas warned. "Just relax. We're going to talk. And if I like what you say, I'll pull you out of there."

Krudd's breathing came in short jerks and his face grew red. Barrabas's fist tightened on his shirt collar. Krudd stopped struggling.

"Please. Please, help me. Please!"

The collar of his shirt ripped and Krudd sank two inches closer to the certain death below. He emitted a moan of terror and tried to be as still as possible. His short little arms hung sideways in case he needed wings.

"I'll tell you where Toto is," he said to Barrabas, wide-eyed and ready to trade favors. "I lied. I know where he is. I'll tell you everything. Just pull me up. Please."

"Where is he?" Barrabas's arm trembled with the strain of the man's weight. He didn't know how much longer he could hold on before he pulled the man out.

Now Krudd saw his advantage.

"Pull me out first," he said. "Please."

His shirt ripped again and Krudd sank even lower. The metal crusher gnashed.

"Where's Toto?" Barrabas snarled.

"At the Voortrekker Monument. Please, lift me out of here!"

Barrabas gripped tighter and wound his fist around the torn cloth. Slowly he started lifting Krudd up. Krudd squirmed in panic, reaching for his arm.

"Uh-uh!" Barrabas warned again. Krudd's arms floated away. "Now tell me exactly. Where's Toto?"

"In an air-raid shelter underneath the monument. There's a door at the back, from the gardens. Please!"

Using his other hand to steady himself on the railing, Barrabas raised his arm and slowly pulled Krudd higher. The diamond industrialist reached out to grab the railing.

His shirt ripped.

Right in two.

A bloodcurdling scream rang through the plant as he fell.

He hit the crushers, looking up at Barrabas with doomed eyes and a last futile call for help.

Too late. He knew his fate.

It was fast.

The crushers swallowed him in one satisfied gulp.

Krudd just disappeared. The metal wheels made a full turn as the conspirator was compacted in the machinery beneath. A pool of blood welled up from the mouth of the crusher like a sick red smile.

The wheels turned. The blood drained back down into the machine, leaving only a faint red grin on the rollers.

Barrabas looked at the torn pieces of cloth still clenched in his fist. He tossed them down to the hungry monster and ran for the helicopter.

18

In the room in the unused bomb shelter below the Voortrekker Monument, Bishop Toto sought comfort in prayer.

He knew that rescue was hopeless. In a few hours, the impostor would be bishop of Johannesburg, and the ensuing riots would destroy the opposition to apartheid for decades.

"Oh, my God," he whispered, on his knees, hands clasped tightly in front of him, eyes pressed shut. "Why have you abandoned me?" Tears tracked their way down his cheeks. More than anything in these, his final hours, he felt betrayed by the God he had spent his whole life serving. His people were so close to victory. Now this! Everything was destroyed by those who wanted to keep millions of African people in servitude.

Where was his God now, he demanded. He wept.

Suddenly, the door flew open with a crash.

A tall muscled man with short white hair and the face of cruel vengeance stood in the entrance and looked at him.

"Bishop Toto?" the commanding voice said.

The bishop looked at him, waiting for the bullets to pound into his brain and his life to seep out. But the big man at the door said only, "I've come to take you to Johannesburg."

AT SUNRISE, the guards at the Krudd estate saw a helicopter descend over the back gardens of the big house.

The sun was still only halfway over the eastern horizon. The sky was baby blue, the air perfumed by the summer morning.

The South African security-force markings on the fuselage threw them off. Two stood by the house. One sauntered across the plush wet grass. Their Belgian FN-FAL autorifles were carefully aimed at the chopper doors.

Not careful enough.

The helicopter suddenly broke from its descent and swung toward the house. The gun kit on the side opened up, and orange fire burst from the muzzles. One of the security men on the terrace ran for the house. Bullets chopped him down. The other aimed his automatic rifle up and pulled the trigger. Too late. His body blew apart from crotch to forehead, and he sloshed to the flagstones.

The one remaining guard stood in the middle of the gardens where he had gone to meet the chopper, alone and exposed.

He tried to run for it.

The chopper descended into a hover outside the house and the soldiers of Barrabas jumped out.

The colonel hit the terrace, rocked to his knees and swirled around, casting a 3-round burst across the grass.

The fleeing guard fell.

Claude Hayes, Alex Nanos and Lee Hatton fanned out from under the chopper as Bishop moved it back to park it on the lawn.

Hayes grabbed the FN-FAL from one of the dead guards while Hatton and Nanos ran for the guardhouse to dispose of troublemakers. Barrabas raised his foot and planted a solid kick to the glass doors that led into the house. They smashed inward, and he and Claude Hayes moved forward.

They ran through the opulent mansion searching for the room where the Inner Circle met. In the foyer, another guard was rushing down the staircase, waving a handgun.

Barrabas gave him good-morning. Three rounds from the Uzi. Hayes backed it up with some old-fashioned 7.62 from the FN-FAL. The gun felt good.

Bits of the crystal chandelier exploded in an icy jangle across the ceiling. The guard on the stairs slammed back into the wall and bounced step by step down the long spiral staircase.

The mercs didn't wait for him to get to the bottom.

They took a doorway that led further into the house, in search of the bloody conspirators.

They spotted the door to the study just as it opened from the inside. Bishop Bloemvaal stood there with Pieter van den Boos right behind him.

Barrabas raised his Uzi and gripped the mag with his left hand. He fired at the jamb overhead and sent a shower of splinters down on the two men. Bloemvaal and van den Boos yelped and jumped back inside, slamming the door.

Hayes's turn now.

He aimed the long barrel of the FN at the lock and blew single shots until the handle fell off. Then he kicked the door open.

Barrabas and Hayes swung inside.

The little white bishop and the gold-mine owner were scrambling to open a window, with the bespectacled Henry Miller and Krudd's baby-faced elder son, Richard, adding to the general confusion. The substitute bishop was right behind them. Richard Krudd turned hysterically and pushed the impostor away, sending the man sprawling by the fireplace.

Barrabas spattered three quick rounds up the wall by the window. Plaster cratered and cracked into dust clouds, and the conspirators jumped and screamed.

"Turn around!" Barrabas roared.

Trembling with fear, they turned, their hands already raised in the air.

"Wh-where's Wilhelm?" van den Boos muttered, his voice quavering.

"He's not coming. Ever again."

The telephone on the side table chimed softly, and Hayes answered. Barrabas nosed his SMG back and forth along the line of the conspirators, as if the Uzi was sniffing for trouble. The little impostor crouched in the corner, his hands folded around his head. He whimpered in terror.

Hayes spoke a few words into the telephone and hung up.

"Hatton and Nanos have secured the front gates."

"Good."

They heard a noise behind them. Someone was walking through the house. It was Geoff Bishop, the pilot, with the real Bishop Toto right behind him.

"All right, gentlemen. Sit!" Barrabas was both triumphant and firm. The members of the Inner Circle looked at one another uncomfortably and slowly took their seats. Barrabas waited patiently.

"Where's Snider?" he demanded when everyone had sat down.

Each conspirator waited for another to speak.

"You!" The colonel jabbed his gun at van den Boos. The gold-mine owner jumped in his seat.

"He's supposed to be here now. He got held up at security headquarters," he answered quickly.

"Good." Barrabas nodded slowly but kept the Uzi's snout circling in front of the man's face. "Phone him."

Van den Boos gulped and gave it a second's thought. He picked up the receiver and pushed the number. He looked at Barrabas and swallowed again.

"Hello. It's Pieter van den Boos. Yes. I'd like to speak to Major Snider. Right away. No. Yes, it's urgent. Immediately, you fool!"

They waited.

"Hello, Sidney. I, er, someone here wants to speak with you. Yes. Nile Barrabas, the American observer," he concluded ruefully.

Barrabas grabbed the receiver away from him.

"Snider, Wilhelm Krudd copped out on you. He told me where to find the real Bishop Toto. So the game is up for you and the Inner Circle."

There was a long silence on the other end of the line.

"You hear me, Snider?"

"Yes," the BOSS major answered slowly, grimly.

"The real Bishop Toto is going to Johannesburg this morning. Not the impostor you and your friends set up for this. Understand?"

Again Snider waited a moment before answering. "I understand," he said finally.

"One more thing, Snider."

"What?"

"We've seized the estate and neutralized opposition here. And we're staying put until the bishop has been consecrated. If anything happens to him, anything, Snider, your fellow conspirators die. One by one. Van den Boos, Bloemvaal, Miller and Richard Krudd. Understand?"

This time there was a long silence. Barrabas waited. He had time to wait.

"I understand," Snider said reluctantly.

Van den Boos grabbed the receiver suddenly from Barrabas. "He means it, Sidney. I'm telling you now! Don't jeopardize us!"

Snider hung up.

Barrabas looked at the Bishop Toto, who waited patiently by the door. His face was pained by what he saw. As a man of the church, he was a man of peace. As a man whose skin was black, he was embroiled in bitter war.

Barrabas didn't like using hostages, either. It left a bad taste, because it was a game that could be turned too easily against them. Innocent people usually ended up getting killed that way. But in the circumstances, he didn't have much choice.

"He didn't make a commitment," Barrabas told Bishop Toto.

"It is a chance I will have to take. You have brought me this far. Now there is another who will protect me."

The telephone rang again, and Hayes answered. He looked at Barrabas and Bishop Toto. "There's a car down at the gates. The men in it claim to be your aides. They're here to pick you up and take you to the cathedral.''

"Let them in," Barrabas said.

Bishop Toto looked around the room before turning to leave. Then he addressed Barrabas. "I thank you for being the instrument of my salvation.''

"It's just a job," Barrabas answered laconically.

"It's much more than that, Colonel. Do you not think that you are just the instrument of a higher good?''

Barrabas smiled and shook his head. "Whatever you say, bishop. I just do what I know is right and I'm always glad to help out. That's all.''

"Then let me ask one more thing from you." The little black bishop shifted his weight and faced the tall American. "If anything happens to me now, to kill these men would be only an act of vengeance. Regardless of what happens to me, when the time is right, let them go.''

"You show a lot of mercy to people who wanted you dead and your people's struggle destroyed.''

"But we cannot defeat them if we remain as evil. My people have a saying. 'Vengeance is a cold fire. Its flames are bright but they give no warmth.'''

"I heard that once," Hayes said, thinking of what Peter Uthulu had said to him. Peter had seen the vengeance burning in Hayes's eyes. Bishop Toto saw it burning in Barrabas's.

"I'll see what I can do," Barrabas said. It was as far as he was willing to go with the Inner Circle looking on. Bishop Toto's eyes met his.

"Thank you.''

"Just remember that saying of yours when your people do finally take power in this country."

"I will. And we will," the famous man answered. He looked up at the door behind the colonel. "Ah. My aides have arrived."

Lee Hatton suddenly appeared with two men both wearing the suits and collars that marked them as ministers. She stood back, her Uzi crossing her chest, to let them into the study.

They greeted Bishop Toto quietly, noticing the strange tension in the hushed room. The little impostor quivered in the corner, his big white eyes wide with fear. But the resemblance to the real Bishop Toto was apparent. The members of the Inner Circle sat in their chairs, their faces whiter than usual.

"Remember what you see here in this room," Bishop Toto told the newcomers. "And I will tell you everything. But now, let us go to the cathedral."

"Good luck," Barrabas said.

Toto turned. This time his eyes twinkled and he grinned. "No luck, Colonel—" he raised his finger as if he was instructing a recalcitrant follower "—the hand of..."

"Yeah, yeah...I know." Barrabas brushed it off. The bishop smiled as he left the room.

Barrabas turned around and eyed the four silent conspirators. His face was dark and grim once again.

"Now," he said. "We wait."

ALMOST SIX HOURS LATER, the voice of Johannesburg's newly consecrated bishop floated from the radio in the study of the Krudd mansion as he made his inaugural speech to the masses assembled outside the cathedral.

Barrabas clicked off the radio and eyed the members of the Inner Circle.

Claude Hayes and Geoff Bishop paced near the windows. The ceremony had come off without a hitch. Barrabas hoped their exit from South Africa would be as smooth. Somehow he doubted it.

"Now are you satisfied?" Pieter van den Boos said bitterly, turning his small accusatory eyes at Barrabas.

"Almost," Barrabas answered. "Geoff, how much fuel is left in the chopper?"

"Couple of hours' worth. Enough to get us out of the country to Mozambique or Lesotho."

The telephone rang and Barrabas picked it up.

It was Snider.

"You've got your Bantu bishop," the security director said derisively. "And I've got something you want."

Barrabas heard the major's receiver being handed to someone. He heard a woman sobbing.

"Colonel Barrabas?" It was Athustra. "They've got Paul and me. We tried to get out but..." She broke down. Snider grabbed the phone back. "Hear that, Barrabas?"

"I heard."

"I'll make you a trade. Van den Boos, Bloemvaal, Wilhelm and Richard Krudd and Miller. For these two."

Barrabas looked over the four members of the Inner Circle. The problems with hostages. It was too easy to turn the tables. "It's a deal, Snider. Except for Wilhelm Krudd. He can't make it. He can't make it ever again."

There was a silence at the end of the line. "Bastard!" Snider said finally. "Where is he?"

"He fell into the crusher at his diamond mine."

On the nearby sofa, Richard Krudd and the others gasped in horror.

"All right, Barrabas. Here's the deal," Snider said tightly. "In half an hour we meet at the Voortrekker Monument to exchange our hostages. You come by car. Afterward I'll see that you get safe passage to the border of Lesotho."

Barrabas thought a moment. He knew the bit about safe passage was crap. But Snider didn't know about the helicopter. "Okay, Snider. It's a deal. On one condition. Your people can close off the road at the bottom of the hill to keep the tourists out. But at the monument, you come alone. None of your agents. If I see anyone, the deal's off. And so are the hostages."

Snider hung up without answering.

19

The sun stood dead center overhead as the long black limousine crawled up the winding driveway that led along the rim of the hill overlooking Pretoria. The massive bulk of the Voortrekker Monument jutted into the sky at the end of the road, its square lines contradicting the gentle rounded contours of hill and sky.

Claude Hayes drove. Barrabas sat beside him in the front. The window to the passengers' section was down. Barrabas was twisted sideways in the seat, keeping his eyes and his Uzi trained on the members of the Inner Circle in the back seat.

The parking lot below the monument was empty, and the road deserted.

"Drive up to the steps," Barrabas told Hayes, pointing to the wide stone staircase that led to the Hall of Heroes.

Hayes slowed the car to a stop in front of the monument, and Barrabas got out and slammed the door. Sidney Snider stood alone at the top of the steps, just outside the main doors. His hand rested on a small but deadly Ingram M-11 SMG—the Uzi's rival for clandestine security work.

Barrabas opened the back door of the limousine.

"Out!" he ordered.

The four members of the Inner Circle and the frightened little African impostor slowly left the car and huddled together. Hayes got out and trained his FN-FAL over the roof of the car at them.

"Here they are, Snider!" Barrabas shouted up to him. "Give me Paul and Athustra."

Snider didn't answer for a moment. He stared down the long flight of stairs, then turned abruptly and disappeared. When he returned he was dragging something. He pushed it down the stairs.

It was a body.

It tumbled limply from step to step like a stuffed doll.

Paul Krudd's corpse came to a stop at Barrabas's feet. A small bloody hole in his temple marked the method of his execution.

Snider had disappeared again. This time he returned to the top of the stairs, holding Athustra by her wrist. The young African woman struggled. He forced her to stand on the top step. She was on the verge of hysteria.

"Paul Krudd for Wilhelm Krudd, Barrabas," Snider announced.

Barrabas felt himself tensing with blind fury, his breath coming in short, sharp jabs. He kept his eyes on Snider. "Let her go," he said.

"Sure," Snider promised. "Her and them. They start walking up. She starts walking down."

Barrabas turned to the defeated conspirators and motioned them forward. They started to climb, almost unsure if they wanted to mount the steps and walk the distance between two men with guns.

The black impostor made up his mind. He turned and bolted for the bushes that grew on the side of the road. Hayes pivoted his autorifle around. "Let him go!'' Barrabas shouted. He kept Snider in view while aiming his Uzi at the Inner Circle. ''Don't any of you try that,'' he warned them. ''Start walking.'' He shoved the snout of the Uzi at the steps.

The South Africans walked.

Snider pushed Athustra forward to the first step. The woman swallowed and cautiously began to descend, barely overcoming the paralysis of her fear.

Hayes walked from behind the limousine.

''I don't like it, Colonel.''

''Me, neither. Something's going to happen any second now.''

''I get that feeling. I just wonder if we should start shooting before he does.''

''How long you think she'll survive?''

''Not long enough to think about it.''

''Hang on another minute.'' Even as Barrabas spoke, he heard the sound far in the distance of an approaching helicopter.

Snider heard it, too. His eyes searched the sky to find its source. The sky was clear, blue and sunny. The helicopter was invisible.

''Barrabas!'' Snider shouted. His voice was on edge, dangerous for a man with a gun.

The four South Africans stopped their nervous ascent.

''Our insurance policy, Snider,'' Barrabas shouted up at the security director.

Athustra continued her descent until she was on the same step as the Inner Circle when the Kiowa barreled around the side of the monument, descending rapidly.

Richard Krudd flipped. He grabbed the black woman. ''She's ours!'' he cried. ''Ours! Back off! All of you! Don't shoot or you'll kill her first!'' He held her in front of him as a shield as he shouted down at Barrabas.

But it was Snider who opened up from behind.

Bullets slammed into Richard Krudd's back. He bowed out like a saucer, his face registering brief surprise and disbelief. He flew face first past Athustra and down the steps.

Then all hell broke loose.

Barrabas fired his Uzi up at Snider, but the security director vanished at the top of the steps, retreating inside the dark doorway that led to the Hall of Heroes.

Van den Boos, Bloemvaal and Miller ran like bats out of hell. They tripped down the steps in a mad panic, racing for the limousine. Athustra froze with fear. Van den Boos grabbed her arm and pulled her after him, with a quick look at Barrabas.

"Get them! I'll take Snider!" Barrabas told Hayes. He took the steps three at a time.

Van den Boos repeated Richard Krudd's ploy, holding the struggling woman in front of him as Miller and Bloemvaal hopped over Paul Krudd's body and ran into the limousine.

"Don't shoot," van den Boos cried, "or you'll kill her." He grabbed her wrist and pulled her toward the car.

Miller took the wheel and started the engine. Just as van den Boos tried to climb in, Athustra twisted her arm from his grip and slammed him in the face. Hayes ran to her. Van den Boos gripped her neck in the crook of his elbow. "Stay there," he shouted, dragging her back into the car. Hayes aimed for the tires and blew off rounds into both front ones.

Miller swerved the big black car around and headed down the drive that led back to Pretoria. Hayes could see Athustra fighting like a tiger in the front seat of the car, but dared not aim at the driver for fear of hitting her. He fired into the car's rear tires. Still it didn't stop. Suddenly the front door opened and two hands pushed Athustra roughly from the moving car.

Hayes ran to help her.

Just then, the Kiowa spun around the monument and descended quickly on a beeline for the escaping auto.

Alex Nanos was handling the controls on the XM-27 miniguns on the side of the helicopter. Bishop leaned the chopper into an angle to give the guns maximum target, and Alex pulled the trigger on the dashboard controls. The XM-27 spat its hot payload into the metal paneling of the limo as it tore down the road. Bullets punctured the back fenders of the car, and Miller, the man at the wheel, panicked.

The tires of the limo screamed as the car went out of control and bounced against the stone guardrail at the edge of the hill. The rear end swung around, turning the car sideways and sending it across the road.

Miller turned the steering wheel to straighten the car and floored the gas at the same time. The bullets in the tires finally did their job. The car didn't respond to the steering wheel. But the engine gulped gas, and the gears caught. The limo surged forward. It hit the guardrail and smashed through, over the edge.

The big limo dived down the hillside and hit the incline fifty feet below head-on, crunching the engine block right up into the driver's seat. The car bounced and seemed to stand vertically for a moment, making up its mind what to do next.

It decided to roll.

It fell forward, crushing the roof into the body of the car. It continued its upside-down slide down the hill, tossing and turning as it bounced from rock to boulder, finally coming to a stop halfway down the hill. A great cloud of dust rose into the air.

As the helicopter chopped its way to a landing, Hayes helped Athustra to the side of the road. The young woman was bruised and in near shock, but finally safe.

He ran to the edge of the hill and looked down at the final tomb of the Inner Circle. The wheels spun lazily in their dust cloud.

Then the gas tank blew.

With a sudden boom, orange flames erupted high into the sky. From the valley below them, where the city of Pretoria lay snug and secure with its tree-lined streets, came the sound of sirens. It was time to go.

The helicopter was setting down at the bottom of the long steps that led up to the Voortrekker Monument.

Hayes ran to find Barrabas.

AS BARRABAS RAN UP THE STEPS of the Voortrekker Monument, bullets pinged along the stone edge of the top step, sending a spray of sharp dust flying into the air. Snider was firing blindly out of the Hall of Heroes. Barrabas rolled sideways along the steps and opened up with his Uzi on full-auto.

He poured a mag inside the dark doors as he rushed the steps and swung into shelter beside the entrance.

The gunfire stopped.

Barrabas discarded his empty mag and rammed a fresh one into the Uzi. He edged over until he was standing by the door. He heard the sound of Snider's shoes pacing on the stone floor far inside the hall.

"Snider, I'm coming after you and I'll come shooting. You want to come out or you want to die?"

There was a long silence from within.

No answer.

Barrabas didn't like no for an answer.

He lowered himself, bending his knees until he was almost squatting. His left hand gripped the Uzi mag, and the finger of his right pressed tightly on the trigger. He counted to three.

He swung straight across the doorway, punching hot rounds of 9mm lead into the cool darkness, then threw himself behind cover on the other side of the door. He flattened himself against the stone wall and listened again.

Silence.

He quickly replaced the mag in the Uzi. This time he was going in.

He gripped the submachine gun and once again lowered himself almost to a crouch.

He whipped around the door and straightened his body into a horizontal forward dive with the Uzi leading. He gave the trigger some hard finger action.

The gun spouted orange muzzle-flashes as a river of lead ripped through the Hall of Heroes. Barrabas sailed forward, hitting the stone floor on his stomach, sending autofire left, right and center. He flipped instantly onto his back and fired more hot lead back at the doorway and the walls behind him.

Bullets ricocheted crazily, spinning and whining their way around the great stone hall and smacking into the giant marble reliefs of the Voortrekkers, frozen in their epic journey across the mountains of South Africa.

No one fired back.

His eyes adjusted from bright sunlight to cool darkness.

Snider was nowhere to be seen.

Barrabas flipped over again onto his stomach. In the massive stone Hall of Heroes, there was only one hiding place.

The great round pit centered in the stone floor under the dome.

"I'm here, Barrabas!" Snider called in answer to the colonel's speculation. The security director was pacing on top of the stone cenotaph set at the bottom of the pit. "I'll tell you what, Barrabas. You come and get me. And if I see your face looking over the edge at me, I'll blow it off, okay?"

A sudden burst of 9mm rounds from Snider's Ingram backed up his words. He fired at the domed ceiling. The bullets chunked on the stone and ricocheted madly back and forth in the hall. The room was a death trap.

The only thing to protect Barrabas from a wayward bullet was luck. And Snider knew that as well as he did.

"Come on, Barrabas. What are the odds that my back will be turned? If my back's turned, you win. You can shoot me. If I see you first, I win. You die. Know what I mean, Barrabas?" Snider let go another burst of SMG fire. Again the bullets chipped against the stone murals and bounced back and forth around the hall.

"Snider, you're crazy!" Barrabas called. "Throw up the gun, and forget about killing."

High-pitched laughter erupted from the opening in the floor. "You Americans are the laughing stock of the world," Snider called angrily when the laughter stopped. "With your hypocritical notions of justice and equality. You're fools, traitors to the white race. We're the ones who brought civilization to South Africa, Barrabas. Us. The white people. This country belongs to us."

"Snider, forget it. Throw up your gun and come out!"

Snider belted out a few more rounds. The bullets spun dizzily around the dome. A ricocheting bullet smacked into the stone floor a foot away from Barrabas, and a spray of fine dust exploded in his face, stinging his eyes.

This was going too far.

Barrabas reached down into the pocket of his pants and felt for the single grenade Nanos had thrown to him the night before. It was still there. He pulled it out. Snider was going to give up, or Snider was going to get it.

"It's a matter of superior genes, Barrabas!" Snider shouted crazily from the pit. "We're better than they are! It's in our white blood! It's justice, Barrabas. Justice!"

To hell with playing games, Barrabas thought.

He pulled himself in a belly crawl across the stone floor until he was almost at the edge of the pit.

"I'll give you justice, Snider!" Barrabas shouted. Blood justice.

It felt good gripping the pin between his teeth and yanking it out.

He counted.

One. Two. Three. Four.

And a little bit.

He tossed it over the edge.

The security man heaved into the air, his body spraying blood as shrapnel tore it to pieces. The lonely Ingram SMG clunked onto the stone floor of the pit. Barrabas stood at the edge and looked down at the

ruined corpse, ripped open across the stone cenotaph. Snider's blood was red.

Like everyone else's.

BARRABAS WALKED SLOWLY OUT OF THE DARKNESS of
the Hall of so-called Heroes into the bright African
sunlight. He held his submachine gun loosely in one
hand. The battle was over. He was drained. For a
moment the dazzling yellow sun hurt his eyes.

At the bottom of the monument, the chopper rested
on the road. Lee Hatton helped Athustra on board,
and Nanos and Geoff Bishop lifted Paul Krudd's body
into the fuselage. Claude Hayes had just reached the
top of the steps. He was out of breath from the run.

"Slow down, Claude." Barrabas told him. "It's
over. We can get out of here."

Hayes heaved a sigh of relief. "There's nothing I
want more. I can't take it here." The black warrior
shifted as he caught his breath, looking out over the
rolling hills of the Witwatersrand and the city of Pretoria spread below them, the grand highways streaming away to Johannesburg and the endless mountains
of tailings from the gold mines that separated the
neighboring cities. "Colonel, slavery doesn't just
mean a man is forced to be someone else's property.
It's when a human being has no power to determine
his own fate, no chance to better himself. This country takes everything away from the black man, leaving him without any power over his own life. That's
why South Africa is a slave state."

"In America we got rid of it a hundred years ago."

Hayes cocked his head. "Twenty. In Selma, Ala-
bama. That was really the beginning of the end. And
look what happened in just twenty years. The same

thing might happen here. But if the South Africans don't smarten up, they're going to lose big."

The two warriors walked down the steps toward the helicopter waiting to fly them to freedom.

"So where to, Claude?"

"Lesotho, Colonel. It's closer. And..." Hayes thought back to everything that had happened in the last few weeks. He thought especially of the good men, black and white, who had fought for justice and died bloody deaths. "I don't want to go back to Mozambique for a while. I'm tired of fighting."

"For now," Barrabas said. He slapped Hayes on the back. The two soldiers ran under the whirling rotors for the final flight to freedom.

MORE GREAT ACTION COMING SOON

SOBs

#10 Vultures of the Horn
by Jack Hild

BIRDS OF A FEATHER...
Buzzards in human form circle the boneyard of famine-struck Ethiopia—Russians, Cubans and Americans. Among these obscene profiteers in apocalypse is a creature Nile Barrabas has been hunting since Vietnam: Karl Heiss. His past crimes forgiven by the CIA, Heiss is back on the agency payroll, pulling the dirtiest of dirty deals. To collect on a long-standing debt of blood and honor, Barrabas and his SOBs go claw to claw with the whole scavenger flock. Birds of a feather stick together, all right—especially after a ride in the Barrabas blender!

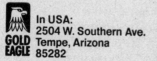